"Hold out y[...] [...]d him over to [...] with a reas[...]

Garrett did as she said, feeling an o[...] [...]ing sense of awe as she settled the babe into his outstretched arms. So, this was what becoming someone's father would have felt like.

"Now bring him to your chest," Hannah coached softly.

As he settled the towel-swaddled infant against his chest, Garrett felt his heart swell.

"I'd like to name him after you," Hannah said, her eyes drifting shut.

Garrett's gaze snapped up, her words taking him by surprise.

"That is, if it's all right with you," she mumbled sleepily.

"I'd be honored," he said. Truth was, he couldn't have been more honored. It wasn't as if he'd ever have children of his own to pass his name down to.

"Garrett Austin," Hannah said with a sigh. Her soft, even breathing told him she had finally fallen into an exhausted slumber.

Garrett looked down at the precious bundle he held in his arms and smiled. "Welcome to the world, Garrett Austin Myers."

Kat Brookes is an award-winning author and past Romance Writers of America Golden Heart® Award finalist. She is married to her childhood sweetheart and has been blessed with two beautiful daughters. She loves writing stories that can both make you smile and touch your heart. Kat is represented by Michelle Grajkowski with 3 Seas Literary Agency. Read more about Kat and her upcoming releases at katbrookes.com. Email her at katbrookes@comcast.net. Facebook: Kat Brookes.

Books by Kat Brookes

Love Inspired

Bent Creek Blessings

The Cowboy's Little Girl
The Rancher's Baby Surprise

Texas Sweethearts

Her Texas Hero
His Holiday Matchmaker
Their Second Chance Love

The Rancher's Baby Surprise

Kat Brookes

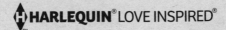

Recycling programs
for this product may
not exist in your area.

LOVE INSPIRED BOOKS

ISBN-13: 978-1-335-53896-3

The Rancher's Baby Surprise

www.Harlequin.com

Printed in U.S.A.

And they that know thy name
will put their trust in thee: for thou, Lord,
hast not forsaken them that seek thee.
—*Psalms* 9:10

I'd like to thank Harlequin for the opportunity I've been given to share my stories with so many of its wonderful readers. It was a dream of mine for a very long time to write for Harlequin, and now I am living that dream. I'd like to thank Melissa Endlich for bringing me into the Love Inspired family, the editing department, my cover artist and Harlequin's fabulous marketing crew. Lastly, I'd like to extend a very warm welcome to my new editor, Carly Silver. Thank you for your time and input with this story. I look forward to publishing many more books with you in the future.

Chapter One

Hannah Sanders eased her foot off the gas pedal as she struggled to make out the winding country road ahead. The overcast day had turned as black as night when she'd driven into the storm. Even her car's high beams struggled to push through the wall of rain before her. Deepening puddles along the barely visible road pulled at her tires, causing Hannah to tighten her grip on the steering wheel even more.

"Dear Lord," she prayed, resisting the urge to run a hand over her rounded abdomen, knowing she needed to keep both hands firmly wrapped about the steering wheel, "please don't let anything happen to this baby." *Her sister's baby.*

The wipers, set on high, pushed water to and fro on the windshield, but the deluge outside rendered them nearly useless. Why hadn't she turned around when she'd seen the approaching storm? As if in answer to her question, the cramping in her lower back returned, this time wrapping around to her swollen abdomen. She hadn't turned around because, according to her GPS, Bent Creek, Wyoming was the closest town in any direction to seek shelter from the storm she was driving through.

Hannah clenched her teeth as the cramping sensation, one she still hoped was nothing more than false labor pains, settled low in her abdomen. Tears pooled in her eyes. "This can't be real labor," she uttered in denial as she fought to push away the sense of panic threatening to overcome her. It was too soon. The baby, the tiny little blessing her older sister and her husband had entrusted her with, wasn't due to arrive for five more weeks. A child that, following the multicar pileup that had taken her sister's and brother-in-law's lives three months earlier, would be Hannah's to raise. To love.

And love this baby she would. With all her heart. He was all she had left of Heather, her only sibling. She told herself to stay calm. That stress wasn't good for the baby, and what she was experiencing was nothing more than false labor pains. But what if they weren't? She couldn't give birth to Heather and Brian's son on the side of some rain-soaked road alone. There could be complications? What if—

A crack of thunder erupted in the looming clouds above just as Hannah started across an old wooden single-lane bridge, yanking her from her fearful thoughts. The Honda Civic shuddered almost violently below her. Then, before she could fully process that the rumble she'd both heard and felt wasn't thunder, the bridge gave way beneath her car.

A panicked cry escaped her lips. She jammed her foot on the brake, not that it made any difference as the nose of her Civic dipped downward. The creek's rampant flow immediately crested over the front end of the hood on the driver's side, mixing with the deluge of rain still coming down around her. Hannah's stomach dropped, and it had nothing to do with the life growing inside her. It was an instantaneous fear of what might very well be her last few moments on this earth. Was this how her sister had felt in the milliseconds before the deadly crash that took her life?

Guilt rose up, overtaking that fear. Her decision to drive on through the storm instead of pulling off onto the side of the road to wait it out would cost her not only her life, but that of the innocent babe she carried inside her. Thick, hot tears of regret rolled down her cheeks. Just when she thought her car was about to be swept away, the rear of the vehicle caught on something, causing it to hang up on the rain-soaked hillside behind her. The car now hung partially submerged in the rushing water of the creek. Thankfully she hadn't been going fast enough for the front air bags to deploy. There was no telling what kind of injury that might have caused to the baby this far along in her pregnancy.

However, the seat belt she'd secured herself in with, thanks to the downward slant of the vehicle, now pulled taut against her swollen abdomen. While it kept her from sliding forward into the dashboard, it also made it harder to breathe and nearly impossible to move.

The engine sputtered and died as water pushed through the partially submerged hood of the car, causing the headlights as well as the inside lighting to go out. Fearing that any movement she might make would dislodge her car from the creek's hillside, Hannah sat perfectly still. If one could call it sitting, with gravity wanting to pull her body downward toward the nose of the car.

Darkness shrouded the world around her as she sat listening to the sweeping rush of the water around her. Rain drummed against the car's roof, the sound drowning out the furious pounding of her heart as the reality of the situation she suddenly found herself in settled into her panic-stricken mind. She was caught up in a flash flood. She'd seen enough news coverage on them over the years to know what they were capable of. Less than two feet of rushing water could sweep vehicles away as if they were nothing more than weightless toys.

A damp chill began to seep into the car, making Hannah shudder. She had to do something. But what if her movement caused the Civic to break free of whatever it was that had hung it up? The car bobbed against the water's force and she knew time was running out. With the water rising as quickly as it was, the flooding creek would soon sweep her—*them*—away. Two more lives gone far too soon.

Her thoughts went to her sister's child and the life he would never have the chance to live. And what of her father? What would become of him? He was still grieving over the loss of his oldest daughter. She couldn't do this to him again. Wouldn't do this to him. Forcing one hand's iron-banded grip to loosen on the steering wheel, she released it and then eased slightly numb fingers across the center console, searching the front passenger seat for her purse and the cell phone she'd left lying on the seat next to it. She only prayed she would have signal out there in the middle of what felt like nowhere.

Her fingertips danced over the empty passenger seat and Hannah groaned. Her purse must have slid onto the floor when the bridge dropped out from under the front of her Honda. There was no telling where her phone had ended up.

"Dear Lord, please keep us safe until help arrives," she prayed, determined to cling to her faith despite the gnawing fear that no one would be out in a storm like this. Why would they be?

She turned her head slowly from one side to the other, trying to assess her situation. Through the heavy downpour, she was barely able to make out the hazy outlines of tree trunks along the creek's bank on either side of her car. Below her, angry whitecaps churned in the rising creek as fallen logs and other debris swirled past.

To think that she'd made the conscious decision to take less-traveled roads on her way back from Idaho to Steamboat Springs, believing the fewer vehicles on the road the safer she and the child she carried inside her would be. She'd been so wrong.

The force of the rising water, surging in a constant push against the side of her Civic, had Hannah's panicked gaze shifting toward the driver-side window. There would be no leaving out that door, which was taking the brunt of the creek's rushing flow. She looked frantically to the passenger side, which, much to her dismay, had water lapping up along its side mirror as well. With no power, she couldn't lower the windows. That left her with only one other option:

getting her very pregnant self into the backseat where she might be able to, if the car remained where it was, make her way out onto the bank of the swollen creek through one of the rear doors. Then she would have to pray she didn't lose her footing on the wet, muddied ground.

The vehicle shifted again beneath her, making Hannah gasp. By the grace of God, it remained where it sat, precariously suspended on the side of the bank. Whatever she was going to do, she needed to do it now. If her car were to dislodge and be taken away by the rushing water, her life would end, right along with that of the innocent baby tucked so trustingly in her womb.

Heart pounding, she moved to unlatch her seat belt. With trembling fingers, she jabbed at the button, but it refused to release. She tried again to no avail. "No," she gasped, a deeper panic setting in. She tried to push free of the strap, but her protruding abdomen made that impossible. Nausea roiled in her gut. Closing her eyes, she tried to calm down. She needed to think.

Another pain, this one sharper than the previous ones had been, caused her stomach to clench. A hazy darkness began to skirt the outer edges of her vision. Hannah's thoughts went to her sister and the babe that should have carried on his parents' legacy. She thought of her widower father back in Steamboat Springs, who would be utterly devastated to lose yet another daughter, another grandchild.

"I'm so sorry," she sobbed softly. Then, letting her fear go, she turned herself over to the Lord's safekeeping as the darkness claimed her.

"I've driven in storms before," Garrett Wade muttered into the phone as he pulled away from his ranch house.

"I'd rather lose a horse than a friend," Sheriff Justin Dawson said worriedly from the other end of the line. Justin, the best friend of Garrett's younger brother Jackson, had property that bordered the Triple W Rodeo Ranch, which Garrett and his brothers shared with their parents. Shortly after the storm had begun, he'd called to ask Garrett for advice regarding one of his mares that was having birthing complications. While he could have possibly talked Justin through the birthing, Garrett felt better seeing to it himself. After all, as a veterinarian, that's what he'd devoted his life to—caring for animals, horses in particular. He'd delivered dozens of foals over the years, and it appeared he'd be adding another to his list that dark and stormy afternoon.

The storm worsened, slowing his travel to what felt like a mere crawl. Rain deluged the windshield of his truck, making it almost impossible to see more than one or two cars lengths ahead. He rounded the curve that cut through one of the smaller wooded hillsides on the property, wondering if he might be better off turning around at the bridge just beyond and help Justin with the delivery of the foal via the phone.

He knew far too well how helpless one could feel when a life hung in the balance. Even if the life in jeopardy that afternoon belonged to a horse. He was still driven to do whatever he could to make certain Justin's mare and its foal survived whatever complications had arisen. As he hadn't been able to with Grace. Not that there was any comparison to the loss of a human life. But if he had the ability to make a difference where he hadn't been able to in Grace's case he would. Be it animal or human.

Grace. It had been a stormy afternoon very much like this one when he'd lost the other half of his heart. His high school sweetheart. No, not lost. She'd been taken from him—by cancer. Seventeen years old, with so much life ahead of her, a life she was meant to spend with him, she had slipped away with him holding her hand.

Pulled abruptly from the painful thoughts of his past, Garrett stepped hard on the brake as he eyed the road ahead. He sent a prayer of thanks heavenward as he took in the sight before him. Had he been traveling any faster, he might not have noticed the bridge had been washed out until it was too late.

The bridge had been old and in need of replacing anyway, but its loss had effectively cut off his family's fastest route into town. Shifting the car into Reverse, he started to back away, preparing to turn his Ford F-450 around and head back to the ranch. However, something protruding from the space where the bridge had once been caught his eye as his truck's headlights passed over it.

Leaning forward, Garrett squinted, trying to make out what that something was through the heavy rain. Part of the bridge, perhaps? He slowly drove toward the creek until the blurred outline became clearer. The moment he realized the back end of a car was jutting up from the sloping hillside, Garrett threw his Ford into Park and jumped out into the rain. Had the vehicle's passenger, possibly even passengers, managed to escape before the car settled so precariously over the rapidly rising creek? Or were they trapped inside, on the verge of being swept away by the swirling water? Heart pounding, he raced toward the collapsed bridge.

"Hello?" he hollered. "Is anyone in there?"

When he received no response, he ran toward the upended vehicle, stopping just far enough away from the creek's edge not to accidentally slip into it. Water was halfway up the front doors, but by some Providence the car's rear held fast against the muddied hillside. Thunder and lightning crashing around him as he pulled his cell from the front pocket of his jeans and switched the flashlight app on. It wasn't as good as having the real thing, but at that moment it cast enough light into the vehicle to see that the Honda wasn't empty. The shadowy outline of a slight female form lay limp against the taut harness of the driver's side seatbelt. He couldn't see her face, as the woman's head faced the opposite direction, but she appeared to be unconscious.

The vehicle creaked and groaned as the rushing water threatened to tear the car free of whatever it was that held it to the bank. His gaze shifted immediately toward the rushing water below as it crested over the car's hood. There was no time to waste. Garrett broke into a run for his truck, heedless of the stinging rain. *Dear Lord, please don't let me have arrived too late.*

He grabbed a heavy-duty flashlight along with the recovery towrope he kept in his truck in case one of their horse trailers got stuck in mud and secured the rope to the front of the F-450. Then he hurried back to where the Honda hung precariously atop the hillside and kneeled on the ground where the back end teetered. Shining the light under the car's carriage, he found a secure place to latch the towrope.

He ran back to his truck. Throwing the over-size vehicle into Reverse, he eased backward until the rope grew taut. Then he gave it a little more gas and began pulling the smaller car back up the bank. It caught for a moment, refusing to budge, which sent Garrett into another round of fervent prayers. Then, as if in answer, it let loose, sliding in the slick mud as it ascended the remainder of the way up the side of the flooding creek.

It wasn't until he'd gotten the car safely away from Bent Creek's rising water that Garrett realized he'd been holding his breath. Exhaling his relief, he grabbed once more for the flashlight and then went to check on the driver inside the other vehicle.

When he reached the car, he pulled on the front door handle, only to find it locked. Aiming the beam of the flashlight directly inside, he saw the unconscious woman now lying back against the seat. A surge of urgency filled him. He pounded on the window as the driving rain beat down on him.

The woman shifted slightly and then her eyes fluttered open. Light green eyes, the color of peridot, looked up at him. The expression on the young woman's face, one of both fear and relief, had him wishing there wasn't a solid metal door separating them. He wanted to tell her she was all right. Needed to know that she truly was all right. Needed his pounding heart to settle back into its normal rhythm.

"You're safe!" he hollered over the storm.

Wide-eyed, the woman looked up at him pleadingly, but she made no move to open the door. Was she suffering from shock? It was understandable if she was. A slender hand rose to flatten against the window in a silent plea and then dropped away as an expression of pain moved across her face. Had she been injured when the car had gone down over the bank?

"Unlock the door!" he instructed, motioning toward the door beside her.

She moved then, just enough to reach for the manual lock button. Then the door clicked.

"Thatta girl," he muttered as he eased the door open. Rain spilled off the brim of his cowboy hat as he leaned in, keeping the beam of the flashlight averted as not to blind her with it. Looking down into her tear-stained face, he asked, "Where are you injured?"

"I'm not," she said shakily.

Maybe she didn't realize she'd been hurt, because there had been no mistaking the pain he'd seen etched across her face as he'd peered down at her through the rain-splattered window.

Before he could respond, she added, "I think I might be in labor."

Labor? She had that part all wrong. Justin's mare was in labor. *She* was recovering from the shock of nearly being swept away by a flash flood. His gaze dropped down to where the shaft of light from the flashlight crossed over her midsection. Her very swollen midsection. *Dear Lord.*

His calming heart kicked up again. "Are you sure?"

"No," she answered with a sob. "But I've been having pains on and off for the past few hours. It's got to be false labor. Please tell me it's false labor," she pleaded, fear in her eyes.

He didn't want her to be afraid. Didn't want her to be in labor, for that matter. Not here. Not now. Memories of that awful, stormy day years before threatened to rush in, but the woman's soft whimper kept Garrett anchored to the present. "When is your due date?" he asked with another glance down at her protruding abdomen.

"Not for five more weeks," she replied, biting at her quivering lower lip.

It was at that moment he realized she was shivering. The inside of the vehicle had grown chilled as it hung partway in the water. The cold rain hadn't helped matters, either, causing that afternoon's temperatures to drop. "Wait here," he told her. "I'll be right back."

"Please don't leave me," she cried out, panic filling her voice.

"I'm going to get my poncho from the truck," he told her. "You're already chilled. We don't need you getting soaked to the bones on top of that."

She eased back against the seat and nodded slowly, another shudder racking her form.

Garrett raced back to his truck, sending up a silent prayer of thanks to the Lord for placing him there when he had. Collecting the oversize poncho, he hurried back to the frightened young woman. *Five more weeks. Please let it be false labor pains and nothing more.*

Opening the car door, he called out, "Slide out and I'll cover you with this." He shook out the folded rain poncho and held it up over himself and the top of the car.

"I… I can't."

His brows drew together. "We're far enough away from the water. It's safe for you to leave your car." But not for a whole lot longer, if Bent Creek kept rising the way it was.

"M-my seat belt is stuck."

"Sit back," he told her. "I'll give it a try."

"Okay," she managed with a weak nod.

Leaning into the car, he reached around the rounded mound of her stomach and jabbed at the release button. Just as she had said, it wouldn't budge. Chilly rain seeped into his clothes as he worked at the latch. Finally, he pulled back with an apologetic frown. "It's not going to give."

Fear lit her eyes. "Are you going to have to leave me here?"

"Not a chance," he said, wanting nothing more than to quell the panic he heard in her voice. "I'm going to cut the seat belt away."

"C-cut it?" she stuttered, the chill she'd taken on seeming to get worse. "Wouldn't oiling the latch be better?"

"I don't have any oil handy," he told her and then with a regretful frown said, "I know you'd rather I didn't damage your car, but with the bridge out and other possible flash floods hitting the area, there's no telling how long it would be before 911 could get anyone out here."

"After having creek water rush through the hood of my car, I think the worst of the damage has already been done."

He nodded in agreement.

Suddenly, her expression changed, her breath catching as her hand moved to the pale yellow shirt stretched taut across her stomach.

"The baby?" he inquired worriedly.

"Yes," she gasped. "Cut the belt," she blurted out. Then, as if suddenly realizing the forcefulness with which she'd made her request, added, "Please."

Hearing the urgency in her voice, Garrett reached into the front pocket of his jeans and withdrew his pocketknife. "I'm coming in from the other side," he said as he stepped back and closed the door, wanting to keep her as dry as possible.

He hurried around and slid into the passenger side, yanking the door closed behind him. Shoving the rain poncho aside, he shifted to face the woman trapped behind the wheel. "Do you think you could hold the flashlight for me? It's heavier than your average household flashlight."

"Y-yes." She reached out to take it from him, holding it firm despite the trembling he'd seen in her hand as she'd done so. With a slight adjustment, she centered the beam on the point where the belt and the latch met. It danced around slightly, but she did her best to steady it.

"Thatta girl," he cooed again, as if talking to a wounded horse. Turning in the seat as much as his long frame would allow, he unfolded the razor-sharp blade. Seeing her tense, he said calmly, "What's your name?"

"H-Hannah. Hannah Sanders."

"Just hold real still for me, Hannah. This should only take a second."

Her gaze dropped to the blade and she swallowed hard. "Y-you didn't tell me your name."

"Garrett Wade," he replied, noting the fear in

her eyes as she looked down at his knife. "No need to worry. I grew up on a ranch." He worked the tip of the knife gently beneath the stubborn strap. "My father taught all three of his sons at an early age how to handle a knife properly."

Her gaze lifted. "How old are you now?"

"Thirty-four," he answered as he focused on the troublesome belt, carefully slicing into it.

She exhaled a sigh of relief. "So you've had lots of time to p-perfect your knife skills."

"Enough," he agreed, her reply causing a grin to tug at his lips.

A scant few moments later, he had freed Hannah Sanders from her restraints. She inhaled deeply, closing her eyes.

Garrett stilled. "You okay?"

Opening her eyes, she met his worried gaze. "Yes. It's just such a relief to be able to breathe fully again."

He nodded in understanding, and then he folded and put away his pocketknife as his racing heart slowed. To think of what might have happened if he hadn't gotten there when he had. "Now we just have to get you somewhere warm and safe."

"Safe?"

He inclined his head toward the creek. "The water's still rising. Best to clear out, just in case it spills over and tries to sweep your car away again."

The look of relief he'd seen on her face faded away with his words.

Garrett silently chided himself for not giving more thought to the words he'd spoken. While they'd been truthful, he supposed he could have kept his concerns to himself. Unlike his brothers, he'd never been any good at saying the right thing when it came to women. Most likely because a majority of his time was spent in the company of animals. Not the best learning ground for social interaction.

"I'm not going to let anything happen to you," he said. "And I'm a man of my word. Now just sit tight while I come around to help you out."

"M-my purse," she said, shivering. "It fell to the floor."

Glancing down by his booted feet, he frowned. "I'm afraid I got mud on it."

"That's okay," she assured him with a weak smile. "It'll wipe clean."

With a nod, he reached for it and then handed it over to her. "I'll be around to get you." Drawing the poncho up over his head, he slipped back out into the storm.

Hannah looked out into the darkness, the flashlight still gripped tightly in her hand. Its beam still directed downward. She watched through the pouring rain outside as her rescuer made his way around the front of her car.

Thank You, Lord, for sending this man to help us. She placed a hand against her stomach, feeling the life stir beneath it. "We're going to be all right, little one." While she didn't know this cowboy who had rescued them, Hannah knew in her heart that he would keep them safe.

Her rescuer stepped up to the driver's side door and eased it open. He had the poncho draped over his head, one long arm holding the outer edge of it over the Civic's roof to help shield her from the rain when she slid out.

Clutching her purse in one hand and the weighty flashlight in her other, Hannah turned, easing a foot out the open door.

"Let me get that," he said, taking the flashlight from her. "Now, careful you don't lose your footing," her said, his words nearly drowned out by the loud pulse of rain hitting the poncho he held extended over them.

Nodding, she pushed to her feet. Only it wasn't the water under her shoes that had her going down. It was her trembling legs which promptly gave way beneath her. The next thing Hannah knew, she was being swept up into a pair of strong arms and carried away from her car and the raging creek beyond.

"I c-can walk," she protested.

"I can see that," came his reply, concern lacing his words. "But I'm not taking any chances. Not when you're having abdominal pains."

"I'm not having them now," she told him, closing her eyes, too exhausted to say any more. When they reached his truck, she expected Garrett to set her on her feet, but he held her securely against him as he opened the passenger door and placed her, as if she weighed nothing at all, up into the spacious bucket seat.

"Don't take the poncho off until I close the door," he told her. "I've got to go unhook the towrope from the truck and then we'll get going."

As soon as the heavy door slammed shut beside her, Hannah worked her way out from under the poncho, her gaze searching the curtain of rain coming down outside for the man God had sent in answer to her prayers. She latched on to his shadowy outline, this kindhearted cowboy who had become her lifeline when she'd thought all was lost. By the time he'd climbed into the driver's seat, Garrett was soaked from his wide-brimmed cowboy hat to his muddied boots. Beneath the fading glow of the truck's dome light, she could see the beads of water dripping from the damp tips of his wet, wavy hair.

"I'm so s-sorry you had to get out in this storm," she said as he reached between them to place his wet cowboy hat onto the floor behind her seat.

"Given the alternative outcome, I thank the good Lord above for putting me in the right place at the right time," he replied as he reached back between the seats to grab a thick woolen blanket. Handing it over to her, he said, "Shove that wet poncho to the floor and wrap up in this. I can hear your teeth chattering from over here."

Nodding, she draped the blanket over herself, relishing the warmth it provided. "I c-can't thank you enough for coming to my rescue." Her hand moved to her swollen belly. "Our rescue."

His gaze dropped to the rounded, blanket-draped mound and then back up to her face. "It's going to be okay. I'm going to take you to my brother's place, where you can warm yourself by the fireplace," he said as he threw the truck into gear. "It's closer than mine. We'll hole up there until the storm lets up. You sure you're all right?"

"I'm alive," she replied with a grateful smile. "I'd say that's far better than all right."

He nodded.

"Do you think your brother will mind?" she asked, the chattering of her teeth easing somewhat as the blanket, along with the heat blasting up from the truck's floor heater, began to ease the chill from her body.

"Jackson?" Garrett said, glancing her way. "Not a chance. The man is a social butterfly. He always welcomes company." He turned the vehicle around and started back along the rain-soaked road.

The warmth filling the truck's cab cocooned her as they drove through the storm. The farther away from the flooding creek they got, the more relaxed she felt. And tired. So very tired. She needed to stay awake. That was her first thought. But, as her eyelids grew heavier, she knew she was fighting a losing battle. While Garrett Wade was little more than a stranger to her, Hannah knew he'd been guided to that washed-out bridge by the Lord in answer to her prayers. He would keep her and the baby she carried inside her safe from the storm outside. Comforted by that knowledge, she closed her eyes and gave in to the exhaustion.

"Are you sure she's only sleeping?"

"She's been through a traumatic experience," a vaguely familiar voice replied. "That sort of thing would wear anyone down."

Hannah struggled to push away the haze of sleep as arms moved beneath her, lifting her. "Garrett?" she said sleepily, trying not to wince as her abdomen suddenly constricted, the pain slightly more intense than it had been before.

"I've got you," he replied.

"You need me to take her?"

"I've got her," Garrett said as he pivoted away from the truck. "Can you see to the door?"

"She doesn't look to weigh much more than a bale of hay. I think my bum leg could have handled it."

"Maybe so, but I promised to see her safely to your place and I intend to do just that."

The passenger door slammed shut behind them as Garrett carried her toward what she assumed was his brother's house, rousing Hannah more fully. She forced her eyes open, her gaze first settling on Garrett and then drifting over to the man keeping pace beside her rescuer. He was holding a large umbrella up over her and Garrett, heedless of the rain soaking into his flannel shirt.

As they neared the house, light from the porch spilled out across the man's face. A face very like the man who held her in his arms. "You must be the butterfly," Hannah said, trying not to show the worry she felt as the possibility that she might truly be in labor settled in.

He looked down at her in confusion and then cast a worried glance in his brother's direction as they ascended the wide porch steps. "Are you sure she didn't hit her head on the steering wheel or something when the bridge dropped out from under her car?"

Garrett hesitated, glancing down at her. "I don't think so."

"I didn't," Hannah replied with a slight shake of her head.

"But you heard what she just called me, right?" the younger man insisted. "Butterfly."

"Oh, that," Garrett said as they stepped beneath the protective covering of the porch roof. "She got that from me," he explained as they crossed the porch. "I said you were a social butterfly," Garrett added in clarification and then added impatiently, "Can you get the door?"

His brother yanked the screen door open and then stepped aside, holding it in place until Garrett had her safely inside the house. Then he followed with a frown. "You couldn't have compared me to something else, like a wolf, for instance?"

Ignoring his brother's muttered complaint, Garrett carried her into one of the rooms off the entryway, where he lowered her onto a large brown overstuffed sofa. Then he kneeled to slide the rain-soaked sneakers from her feet. "Best get these wet shoes off you." He glanced back over his shoulder at his brother. "Got a thick pair of socks she could borrow?"

"Be right back," his brother said.

"I don't need..." she began, but he was already moving through the entryway in long-legged strides, his gait somewhat off.

"Yes, you do," Garrett said firmly as he set her wet shoes aside and then adjusted the bottom of the blanket to cover her stockinged feet. Then he stood and took a step back. "You can't afford to catch a chill."

Too tired to argue, she said, "No, I suppose not."

His brother hurried back into the room, a thick pair of wool socks in hand. "These might be a little big on you, but they'll be plenty warm."

She reached for them. "Thank you."

"If you haven't already figured it out," Garrett said as she removed her socks and pulled on the pair she'd been given, "this lanky cowboy beside me is my brother Jackson Wade. Jackson—" his introduction was cut off as Hannah let out a soft gasp. His worried gaze shot to her face. "Hannah?"

She sank back into the sofa, a hand pressed to her swollen belly. "It's okay," she said shakily. At least, she prayed it was.

"Another pain?" he asked with a frown.

Jackson's gaze dropped to the blanket covering the rounded swell of her stomach and his thick brows shot upward, clearly noticing her condition for the first time since she'd been carried in. "Is that... I mean is she...?"

"Pregnant?" Garrett finished for him. "Yes. And, despite her reassurance otherwise, I think she might be in labor." He looked down at her. "Hannah? Should I call 911?"

His brother's eyes snapped up, some of the color leaving his tanned face. "Labor? As in, having her baby right now?"

Dear Lord, I hope not. Hannah shook her head, refusing to believe that was the case. "I don't think there's any need to do that. I've been under a lot of stress lately. And then getting caught up in that flood, well, I'm sure they're just false labor pains. I'm not even close to my due date yet."

Jackson looked relieved. Garrett, on the other hand, didn't appear to be as accepting of her reply.

"We should call your husband," Garrett said. "Let him know you and the baby are safe."

"I'm not married," she replied.

"I see," he said with a quick glance at her rounded abdomen.

Warmth blossomed in her cheeks. "The baby's not mine." The second the words left her mouth she realized how untrue they were. The child growing inside her womb was hers now, for as long as the good Lord willed it to be.

The two men exchanged glances. Not that she blamed them. She knew how that last statement had to sound to them.

"The baby was my sister's," she explained, tears filling her eyes. "She and her husband had tried for so long to have a child, but she could never carry to term. So, when the doctor suggested they look into finding a gestational surrogate to carry their baby for them, I knew I wanted to do this for her."

"*Was* your sister's?" Garrett replied with a gentle query.

Her hand went protectively to her stomach as she choked out the words, "Heather and Brian died three months ago in a car accident."

"Hannah," Garrett groaned. "I'm so sorry."

She brushed a stray tear from her cheek. "I'll manage."

"Alone?"

"Women raise children alone every day." She ran her hand over her stomach, a knot forming in her throat. "This child is all I have left of my sister. I'll do whatever it takes to make his life one filled with love and happiness."

"Is there someone else we could call for you?" Jackson asked.

Her gaze dropped to the floor between them. "No."

"No one?" Garrett pressed worriedly.

"It's just my father and me, and he's been really sick with a virus. Probably brought on by all the stress of dealing with my sister's recent death," she said. "It's been so very hard on him. Especially since we lost my mother a little over a year past. I won't have him worrying himself even sicker over me when I'm perfectly fine. Just carless."

Garrett nodded in understanding, yet the worried frown remained fixed on his handsome face. "We'll see what we can do in the morning about getting your car out of there."

"If it's still there," she said with a shudder.

"Either way," he agreed, "it's not going to be drivable. You'll be needing a rental car to get back to…"

"Steamboat Springs," she supplied.

"You're a ways from home," Jackson said.

Hannah felt another twinge starting. *Please, oh, please, make it stop.* "There was something I needed to do," she said, trying to keep her voice calm when she felt the panic washing over her. "If you don't mind, I'd like to freshen up a little bit." And take a moment alone to collect herself. Stress wasn't good for the baby and she'd been under so much of it. Was it any wonder she was experiencing premature labor pains?

Jackson motioned toward the doorway. "Take a left down the hall. The bathroom will be the second door on your right. In the meantime, can I offer you something to drink?"

"I think I might have a few packets of tea left in the cupboard," Jackson replied. "Can I fix you a cup of chamomile tea?"

"It would help to take the chill off," she said, another sharp pinch squeezing at her abdomen. Maybe she should ask Garrett if he could drive her to the hospital once the rain slowed, just to be sure she wasn't in true labor. "But I hate to impose on you any more than I have already."

"You're not imposing," he replied. "I like having company. I'm a social butterfly, remember?" he said with a glance in Garrett's direction, causing his brother's mouth to quirk in a barely suppressed grin. Then he turned back to Hannah. "That being the case, I just wish we had been able to meet under better circumstances."

She nodded. "Agreed." When the viselike grip took hold of her stomach, Hannah fought the urge to groan aloud. Shoving aside the blanket Garrett had lent her in the truck, she made a quick adjustment to the leather strap of her purse, securing it atop her shoulder as she pushed awkwardly to her feet.

Garrett reached out to steady her.

"Thank you."

"Do you need me to walk you down the hall?"

Shaking her head, she lifted her gaze to meet his. "There's no need. I'll be fine."

"I don't think—" he began, only to be cut off by his brother.

"Why don't we go fix that tea Hannah said she'd like to help take the chill away?"

"It doesn't take two of us to make a cup of tea," Garrett argued with a frown.

His younger brother arched a warning brow.

Reluctantly, Garrett stepped aside, watching worriedly as Hannah made her way past him and out of the room.

"I'll tell you right now," she heard him say as she walked away, "The cowboy in me doesn't like leaving her to fend for herself in her condition. Not one little bit."

Thank the Lord for cowboys. If not for men like Garrett Wade, she might have lost more than her own life. She would have lost the baby Heather had prayed so long for.

Chapter Two

Garrett glanced up from where he sat at the edge of the sofa, waiting on Hannah's return, when his brother came back into the room carrying a steaming ceramic mug.

Jackson glanced around. "Not back yet?"

"No," he muttered with a frown, his gaze moving past his brother to the entryway.

He followed the line of Garrett's gaze with a deepening frown. "Maybe you should go check on her."

He wanted to. Would feel a whole lot better if he did. But Hannah had assured him that she was fine. He had to take her word for it. "Best give her a little time," he told his brother. "She's been through quite an ordeal. I'm sure she just needs a little extra privacy to sort through all of her emotions."

"You're probably right," Jackson agreed with

a nod as he placed the mug onto the coffee table and then settled into a nearby recliner.

Garrett sat staring at the paper tag that dangled over the rim of the stoneware cup as the tea steeped. Rain pinged against the windowpane as the storm continued on outside. Beside him, the clock over the fireplace mantel ticked away the minutes. Too many minutes. What if Hannah's legs had given out on her again? What if she'd fainted from all the stress she'd been under? Losing her sister and brother-in-law, suddenly finding herself in the role of mother-to-be, nearly dying in a flash flood.

"Maybe I will go check on her," he announced and was just about to shove to his feet when Hannah, face alarmingly pale, stepped into the doorway.

The sight of her wan complexion and fearful eyes had both men shooting to their feet.

"Hannah?" Garrett inquired as he moved toward her.

She looked up at him, tears in her eyes. "I think my water just broke."

It took a moment for her words to sink in. *Dear Lord.* "You think?" Maybe she was mistaken.

"I'm pretty sure it did," she said shakily.

He crossed the room to where she stood

trembling. "Everything's going to be okay." He prayed he sounded more confident than he felt at that moment.

"I'll call 911," his brother said as he pulled his cell phone from his jeans pocket.

"I'll take her to the guest room," Garrett replied with a worried frown as he scooped Hannah up into his arms, using the utmost of care. Since her water had broken, he thought it best she not walk around.

She trembled against him as he carried her back down the hall to one of the guest rooms.

"I'm so sorry," she said against his shirtfront with a hiccupping sob.

"There's nothing to be sorry about," he assured her as he lowered her quaking form onto one of the twin beds lining the walls. "Are you in pain?"

"Not at the moment," she choked out as she curled up on her side.

"But you're still having contractions?" he deduced.

"Yes," she confirmed, tears streaming down her cheeks. "And they're coming closer together."

He didn't have the means to stop, or even slow her contractions. And with her water having broken, there was no turning back. Hannah was having her baby whether she was ready for it or not. "Looks like you're about to bring that little one into the world. We'll need to start timing them."

Her hand shot out, grasping at the sleeve of his shirt. "He can't come yet. It's too soon."

"Babies come early sometimes," he said calmly when he was anything but. Still, he felt the need to say something, anything, to ease the fear he saw in those large, green eyes of hers. "They just need a little extra seeing to. As soon as the ambulance gets here..." he began, the words drifting off as her troubled gaze left his. Garrett turned to see his brother standing in the open doorway, looking nearly as pale as Hannah had only moments before.

"There's a tree down across Miller Road," his brother said evenly. "No through traffic."

"We've got chainsaws," Garrett said determinedly. "We can see to it."

"Please don't leave me," Hannah blurted out, her grasp on his shirtsleeve tightening.

Jackson stepped farther into the room, shaking his head. "We won't." He looked to his brother. "Can't actually. The tree brought several wires down with it, some of which are hot. The electric company is sending out an emergency crew. Once that's been taken care of, the tree can be safely cleared away and the ambulance can get through. Until then..." He let the words trail off.

"We're on our own," Garrett muttered in understanding.

Another gasp pushed through Hannah's pinched lips, drawing both men's gazes her way.

"Aren't you going to do something?" Jackson demanded of his brother.

Garrett forced his gaze to his brother. "Me?"

Jackson glanced over at Hannah, his expression one of concern. "You're a doctor. Help her."

"You're a doctor?" Hannah repeated, sounding so hopeful.

He shot his brother a chastising look before turning back to Hannah. "I'm a veterinarian. The only babies I have ever delivered are the four-legged kind." He glanced back over his shoulder. "Jackson, head on over to Mom and Dad's and let them know what's going on. Bring Mom back with you. If anyone knows about birthing babies, it's her." She had chosen to deliver her two youngest sons at home with only the help of Mrs. Wilton, a friend of his mother's who was a midwife.

"Garrett, I would never forgive myself if they got caught up in a flash flood on their way back here to help me."

"They'll be fine," he assured her. "Go," he said to Jackson. As soon as his brother took his leave, Garrett turned back to Hannah. "Our parents live just a short distance up the road in the direction opposite from the rising creek."

"Jackson will have Mom back here in no time. In the meantime, we'll need to give your ob-gyn a call to let him know what's going on."

"Her," she said with a soft sniffle. Releasing the hold she probably hadn't realized she still had on his sleeve, she reached into her purse to retrieve her phone. Her hands were trembling so hard, it appeared to be all Hannah could do to hold on to it as she brought up her contact list. She lifted her gaze to his. "Would you mind calling for me?"

He reached for the phone and glanced down at the names on the screen. "Dr. Farland?"

"Yes. That's her," she said.

As he made the call, Garrett prayed the Lord would continue to keep her and her unborn child safe. He had told her everything would be all right, but that decision lay in far greater hands than his own.

"Garrett?" he heard his mother call out as Jackson's front door banged open. Scurrying footsteps followed.

He looked up from where he sat in a chair next to Hannah's prone form to see his mother, followed by Jackson, spill into the room, twenty minutes after his brother had gone to get her.

Hannah, whose long, dark russet hair now hung in sweat-dampened ringlets around her face, accentuating her large, pain-filled eyes, attempted to sit up.

"Don't get up on my account," Emma Wade immediately protested with a staying hand as she crossed the room. Then, after taking a good look at the woman Garrett had rescued from near tragedy, said, "You must be Hannah."

"Yes."

"Such a pretty name." With a warm, motherly smile, she introduced herself.

Hannah nodded, unable to speak as a groan slid past her tightly compressed lips.

Garrett couldn't suppress his worried frown as he looked up at his mother. "Her pains are coming about six minutes apart."

"Then I'm here just in time to take over," his mother said, giving his arm a comforting pat.

"I'll just wait out on the front porch," Jackson said as he backed out through the open door.

Garrett started to stand, to join his brother, but Hannah latched on to his hand, her grip firm. He glanced down to find glistening, fear-filled eyes staring back at him, and he couldn't bring himself to leave her side.

"It's going to be okay," he said, giving her

hand a comforting squeeze. Just then, thunder rumbled outside, rattling the windowpane and Garrett was pulled back to the past.

"I'm scared."

"You're going to be okay, Grace. I won't let anything happen to you," he promised. And then she was gone.

A firm hand came to rest on Garrett's shoulder, pulling him back to the moment. "Honey," his mother said softly beside him, "I'll see to Hannah now. Why don't you go wait with your brother and watch for the ambulance to get here? They might get the road cleared sooner than expected."

He looked to Hannah, torn between the need to stay with her and the need to distance himself from the bad he knew could happen so unexpectedly.

"It's okay," Hannah said, slowly slipping her hand from his. "I'll be fine." She sent an appreciative smile to his mother.

If it was *okay* then why did he feel like he still needed to do more?

Before Garrett could respond, Autumn, new bride of his youngest brother, Tucker, stepped into the room. "Water is heating on the stove."

"Thank you, honey," his mother replied.

"Jackson called you and Tucker, too?" Garrett asked with a frown.

"He didn't call them," his mother replied as she returned to Garrett's side. "I did. I thought it would be good to have another woman here to help out, just in case the ambulance hasn't arrived by the time Hannah's little one is ready to make his grand entrance into the world."

"And Blue?" he asked, referring to his niece, Tucker's little girl.

"Is back at the house, coloring with her grandpa," Autumn answered.

"Hannah, honey," his mother said, "this is my daughter-in-law, Autumn."

"I'm so sorry you all had to come out on a day like this," Hannah said, tears filling her eyes. Before either Autumn or his mother could reply, she gasped, and then clutched at the mound beneath the blanket he'd covered her with while they had waited for his mother to get there. Her pretty face contorted in pain, and her breaths became panicked, coming short and fast.

His mother nudged him from the chair. "Time for you to go join your brothers out on the porch."

He nodded and stood, knowing his mother was right. He needed to leave the room, but it was killing him to do so. His gaze moved once more to Hannah and the pain he saw there grabbed at his heart. *Lord, please find it in Your heart to ease her pain.* He looked to his mother. "Call me if you need my help."

"I will," she said calmly.

"Garrett," Autumn said softly from behind him.

He turned to look at his sister-in-law.

She offered a calming smile and said in that sweet, Texas-accented voice, "Your momma and I are gonna take real good care of Hannah and her little one."

"Honey," his mother said as she settled into the chair he had just vacated, "ask Jackson if he has a hair dryer. I don't want Hannah catching a chill with her damp hair. We're going to be needing some clean towels, and something to cut and then clamp the umbilical cord with. Sterilize them with rubbing alcohol, if your brother has a bottle of it on hand. And please ask Jackson to bring us that water Tucker put on the stove to boil."

"I'll see to it," he replied, grateful to have something to do other than just stand around wondering when the ambulance was going to get there. He just prayed it would be soon.

"Thanks for calling to let me know," Garrett said, relieved to hear that Justin had been able to help his mare deliver her foal safely into the world. Now he just prayed Hannah would be able to do the same with her baby.

"Keep me updated on Miss Sanders," Justin

said. "In the meantime, I'll see to it the road to the washed-out bridge is closed."

"I will," Garrett said, ending the call. Then he turned and started back across the porch, shoving his cell back into the pocket of his jeans.

"You're going to pace a hole right through my porch floor," Jackson grumbled as Garrett passed by the rustic wooden chair in which his brother was seated.

Tucker nodded in agreement from where he sat stretched out in the matching high-back bench. "If he paces any faster, the floorboards are likely to spark into a trail of flames."

How could his brothers just sit there, sipping at their coffee and making jests as if it were just another ordinary day? It wasn't. Truth was, riding bulls and climbing atop broncs during his rodeo days had been less nerve-racking then this. "Do either of you realize how serious this situation is?" Garrett demanded as he continued pacing. "It's not time for her baby to come." He looked toward the door. "I should be in there with her."

"She's in good hands," Tucker said soberly.

"Best thing you can do for her right now is pray," Jackson suggested.

"And what if those prayers go unanswered?" he asked, as they hadn't been with Grace. "Hannah's too young to die."

"Hannah isn't going to die," Jackson said firmly. "She's young and healthy."

"She's been in labor for nearly three hours."

"Babies come out when they're good and ready," Tucker replied, "If God planned to call Hannah home, He wouldn't have seen to it that you were there to save her and the child she's carrying from those flood waters."

He prayed his brother was right. Yet, despite his brother's reassuring words, Garrett couldn't quell the restless energy that filled him. So, he continued pacing the length of the porch which ran all the way across the front of the cedar-sided ranch house.

The front screen door creaked open, bringing Garrett's steps to a halt and drawing all three men's gazes that direction. Autumn stepped out onto the porch and Garrett swallowed hard. It had only been forty-five minutes since he'd left Hannah in his mother's and Autumn's safekeeping, minutes filled with searching glances toward the distant road for an ambulance that had yet to arrive, minutes filled with anxious pacing and fervent prayers. Why wasn't his sister-in-law still inside helping his mother? Unless...

Garrett's heart thudded as he zeroed in on Autumn's face. Hannah had said herself that it was too soon for her baby to be born. Not that babies didn't arrive early all the time, but usually they were delivered in a hospital with medical equipment readily available to care for a premature baby. His fears were laid to rest the moment he realized that his sister-in-law was smiling.

"Hannah?" Garrett asked, the word coming out of a raspy croak.

"Tired, but doing well."

Jackson sat upright and pushed to his feet. "And the baby?"

"He's tiny," she said, and then seeing Garrett's worried frown, added, "but that's to be expected seeing as how he came early. And he's breathing on his own."

"Thank the Lord," all three men muttered in unison.

"No sign of the ambulance?" she asked.

"Not yet," Tucker answered with a shake of his head.

A slight frown pulled at her lips at hearing that.

"I'll call and see if I can find anything out," Jackson offered.

"That would be good," she said with a nod. Then she looked to Garrett. "Hannah's asking for you."

"She is?" he said, feeling a surge of something he couldn't explain move through him. And then, without waiting for a reply, he hurried into the house. Long strides carried him down the hallway to his brother's guest room. He needed to see for himself that Hannah was all right. That her baby was all right.

His mother looked up from where she sat watching over Hannah when he stepped into the room. "Perfect timing," she said with a smile as she rose from the chair. "I'm parched. While you sit with Hannah and her little one, I'm going to go fix Autumn and myself a cup of tea and call your father."

Garrett looked to the bed where Hannah lay, her face blessedly pain-free. She looked tired—understandably, after all she had been through—but there was a glow about her that hadn't been there before. Her long hair, now dry with the exception of a few sweat-dampened spirals, fell about her face and down over her shoulders. It was the most vibrant shade of copper-red he'd ever seen, reminding Garrett of a fall sunset. Something he hadn't picked up on in the dark of the storm.

His gaze fell to the towel-wrapped bundle Hannah held in her arms as she lay there and the tiny face peeking out of it. So very tiny.

"He doesn't bite," Hannah said with a sleepy smile as she looked down at the babe in her arms. "You can come closer."

"He's perfect," Garrett said in awe as he moved to settle into the straight-backed chair his mother had just vacated. Despite his slightly wrinkled, blotchy red skin and scrawny little limbs, her son was perfect. The baby had a dusting of strawberry blonde hair on his head and big, slate blue eyes.

"He's so small," Hannah said with a worried frown as she looked down at her son. Then her gaze lifted to meet Garrett's. "But he's here. Without you, he might have..." Tears filled her eyes. "We might have..."

"But you didn't," he said, not wanting her to dwell on what could have happened. It hadn't. "And I think the Lord played more a part in it than I did," he added with a warm smile.

"That might be the case," she agreed. "But you were the one He sent to save us. The man who risked his own life to save ours. The man who helped to calm me, finding us shelter during the storm. I can never thank you enough for what you did for us."

"Seeing that you're both all right is enough for me," he said, noting that she could barely keep her eyes open.

"I should leave you to rest," he said.

"I'm so tired," she admitted with a soft sigh.

"Then close your eyes and get some sleep," he told her.

Worry creased her brows. "I don't dare. Not

while I'm holding him. He could fall from my arms if I relaxed in sleep."

"I could hold him for you," he heard himself offering before he thought things out thoroughly.

"If you don't mind," she agreed with a sleepy yawn. "I know he'll be safe with you, and I'll only close my eyes for a short while."

She was trusting the most precious thing in the world to her into his safekeeping. Garrett's gaze came to rest on the sweet face of her newborn son. He was so small. Hardly bigger than his own outstretched hand, he thought with a surge of panic. Not that he hadn't handled other small newborns before, but those had been in the form of bunnies and puppies and kittens. *This* was a baby, and he would never have one of his own.

"Garrett?"

He looked up at Hannah. "I've never held a baby before. I'm not sure I would even know how to go about it."

"That's how I felt when your mother laid him in my arms. But it's much easier than you think," she said with a reassuring smile. "But you'll need to wash your hands first."

Of course. He knew that. He should have done so before ever coming into the room, but he'd been so eager to see for himself that Hannah and the baby were all right. "Be right back," he said, hurrying off to the washroom.

When he returned, Hannah smiled up at him. "Ready?"

"Ready."

"Okay, now hold out your arms and I'll hand him over to you."

He did as she said, feeling an overwhelming sense of awe as she settled the babe into his outstretched arms. So, this is what becoming someone's father would have felt like.

"Now bring him to your chest," Hannah coached softly. "It will help to keep him warm. Just make sure his face isn't covered. He doesn't have as much body fat on him as a full-term baby would have had."

As he settled the towel-swaddled infant against his chest, Garrett felt his heart swell.

"I'd like to name him after you," Hannah said, her eyes drifting shut.

Garrett's gaze snapped up, her words taking him by surprise.

"That is, if it's all right with you," she mumbled sleepily.

"I'd be honored," he said. Truth was he couldn't have been more honored. This child she'd given birth to was all she had left of her sister and he was going to carry Garrett's first name. And it wasn't as if he'd ever have children of his own to pass his name down to. His heart had died with Grace that day, along with his dreams of having a family of his own.

"What's your middle name?"

"Austin," he replied, his attention centered on the tiny face before him.

"Garrett Austin," Hannah said with a sigh. Her soft, even breathing told him she had finally fallen into an exhausted slumber.

Garrett looked down at the precious bundle he held in his arms and smiled. "Welcome to the world, Garrett Austin Sanders."

He sat holding the infant for nearly half an hour, his mother and Autumn popping in and out to check on Hannah who was still sound asleep. Both had offered to take the baby, but he'd refused to part with the sleeping infant. While holding something so small—a living, breathing little something—terrified him, Hannah had entrusted him with her baby's safekeeping. He would keep her son cradled in his arms until she awakened.

That determined thought had no sooner passed through his mind when the sound of the baby's breathing changed. Not significantly. If he hadn't been holding the bundled infant against his chest, he might not have even noticed. But it had definitely quickened, the urgent little breaths enough to stir unease in his gut.

He crossed the room and stepped out into the hallway. "Mom," he called out softly, not wanting to startle the baby.

A second later, she was in the hall, moving toward him. "Honey? Is something wrong?"

"I'm not sure," he answered with a worried frown as he looked down at the baby. "His breathing seems a little off. I wanted to see what you thought before overreacting." Preemies might have issues with underdeveloped lungs, but that wasn't always the case.

Concern lit her features as she leaned in to check on Hannah's son. That concern remained as she lifted her gaze back up to his. "His coloring doesn't look good. We need to get him some immediate medical care."

Care that Garrett couldn't provide. "Take the baby and have Autumn get Hannah ready to leave." He started for the front door.

"What are you going to do?" she called after him.

"Whatever it takes," he answered as he let himself outside.

Minutes later, Hannah was lying across the backseat of his truck, her newborn son held securely in her arms as they drove across the range, along the fence line that ran parallel to the temporarily impassable road. He hated that they didn't have a car seat for her son, but there was no time to wait for the ambulance to be able to get through. Jackson and Tucker had gone on ahead of them to take down a section of the fence for them to drive through in order to safely access the road beyond the downed wires.

"Garrett," Hannah said, "I'm scared."

That made two of them, but he wasn't going to tell her that. "We'll be at the hospital before you know it. Tucker's calling to let them know we're on our way." He followed his words of assurance up with a silent prayer. One for the baby and one for himself, because he was going to have to step through those dreaded hospital doors.

They were met by hospital personnel with a wheelchair for Hannah at the emergency room pull up. Her son, now laboring for breath, was quickly whisked away ahead of them. Hannah looked up at him, tears in her eyes.

He squeezed her hand reassuringly. "It's going to be all right."

As soon as she was settled, the hospital attendant wheeled her in through the automatic sliding doors.

Garrett, heart pounding, nausea roiling in his stomach, stood staring at those same doors as they slid shut behind the departing wheelchair. Hannah needed him. But so had Grace. *Please, Lord, let us have gotten here in time.*

Gathering his courage, more courage than

he'd ever needed back when he was riding bulls and broncs professionally, Garrett followed them inside.

Chapter Three

Fighting a yawn, Garrett pulled out his cell phone to check the time—9:37 a.m. He wondered if Hannah had awakened yet. The previous day's events had clearly left her spent, and understandably so. And what about her son? Lord, he prayed the infant that he'd held in his arms shortly after his birth was faring well. The emergency room personnel had taken him straight to the neonatal intensive care unit as soon as they'd arrived at the hospital and he hadn't gotten to see the baby again before he'd left to head home.

Hannah hadn't been the only one under emotional stress when they'd arrived at the hospital the day before. Garrett hadn't stepped foot inside the place since the day Grace had taken her last breath there. Truth was, he dreaded ever having to return there again, but none of that had mattered when Hannah's son's life was at stake.

Once Hannah had been examined, she'd been placed in a private room just down the hall from the NICU. Garrett had then done his best to calm her fears, pushing his own aside. Despite the doctor's reassurance that it was common for a baby born five weeks earlier than expected to need a little help breathing, that his lungs would strengthen in the days and weeks ahead, she'd been beside herself. So much so, that Garrett had ended up staying by Hannah's bedside until late into the night, talking to her about anything and everything to keep her mind from going into the dark places he knew all too well. Places he'd gone to when Grace had taken a turn for the worse, with all the whys and what-ifs.

Exhaustion threatened to drag him down. He had remained seated at Hannah's bedside the night before until sleep had finally claimed her. And that hadn't been until well after midnight.

"Morning," Garrett muttered as he stopped by the corral on his way to the barn.

"Morning," Tucker replied. His brother stood in the center of the corral, working with a green mare they'd purchased to use as a saddle horse. Breaking in horses was one of his brother's specialties. "Didn't expect you in this early. Not after the late night you put in."

Garrett raised a brow. "How did you know about that?" He'd been in touch with his family from the hospital to update them, but he hadn't called anyone when he'd finally headed home. It had been too late.

"Couldn't sleep," his brother admitted. "I was sitting on the porch when you drove past. How was Hannah doing when you left?"

"As well as can be expected, under the circumstances." Garrett glanced around, seeing their other brother's truck parked beside the far end of the barn. "Where's Jackson?"

"In the barn," Tucker replied, his gaze remaining fixed on the young mare. "Just got back from running feed out to the veteran horses."

Unlike a lot of rodeo stock companies that unloaded their retired stock once the animals' profitability was gone, the Triple W Rodeo Ranch kept theirs. They had a special section of land fenced off specifically for the older horses where they could live out the remainder of their lives in leisure, being grain-fed daily. They had worked hard during their rodeo years. In his opinion and his brothers', they deserved no less.

Garrett nodded, not that his brother had seen him do so. Tucker's visual focus remained solely on the mare he was coaxing to pick up her pace as she ran around the outer edge of the fenced-in enclosure.

Shoving his phone back into his jeans, he

leaned against the fence, watching his little brother at work.

"Didn't expect to see you here this morning." Jackson's familiar voice came from behind him.

Garrett glanced back over his shoulder to see his brother striding toward them. "Why wouldn't I be here?"

"You having had such a late night and all," his brother prompted.

Garrett's gaze shifted back to Tucker.

His youngest brother must have felt his accusing stare, because there was no way Tucker could have seen it with his back to them the way it was. Yet he called back over his shoulder, "I might have mentioned to Jackson that there was a good chance you'd be hitting Snooze on your alarm clock today."

"Well, I didn't," he said in irritation. At thirty-four he could still manage a late night here and there and still get up in time to help his brothers with ranch duties. How was he supposed to sleep in, anyhow, with thoughts of Hannah and her son weighing so heavily on his mind? "I have blood draws to do today."

Every six months, they needed to draw blood from the rodeo stock to keep their health certificates up-to-date. Otherwise, they wouldn't be able to transport the broncs from state to state to the various rodeos. Having an in-house vet on the ranch also saved them money.

Jackson lifted a brow. "Someone's a little on the touchy side this morning."

"Maybe a little," he grumbled. "Lack of sleep, and then receiving some bad news, has a tendency to bring that about."

Jackson's head snapped around. "Hannah?"

He shook his head. "No. She and the baby are okay. Or, at least, they were when I left the hospital last night. The bad news is business related."

That grabbed both of his brothers' attention.

"Kade called this morning," he explained. "He had to put Little Thunder down last night." Kade Owens owned the Breakaway Ranch in Oklahoma where, along with raising beef cattle, he bred and raised bucking bulls. Little Thunder was one of Kade's top, prize-winning bulls. The Triple W had partnered up with Kade a few years back to allow them, as a joint partnership, to qualify for a PRCA stock contractor card, which required the stock provider to own a minimum of twenty-five bareback horses, twenty-five saddle bronc horses and twenty-five bulls.

"What happened?" Tucker asked.

"Thrombosis of the inferior vena cava."

"Which is what?"

"A liver abscess," Garrett explained, "which led to a serious infection near the heart."

Jackson shook his head. "A real shame. He's been a good bull. Hopefully, The Duke and Wise Guy will come into their own this year."

"They showed promise last season, so maybe this will be their year," Garrett acknowledged with a nod, recalling the two newest additions to Kade's rodeo bull lineup. "At least, Kade still has some top contenders that rank right up there with Little Thunder for the upcoming season." Their first scheduled rodeo fell during the second week of June. Without having promising stock to offer for rodeo competition, contractors risked losing out on future contracts. That's why they made sure their stock stayed strong and healthy, sending the best they had to offer out to the various rodeos.

"True," Jackson agreed with a nod as they watched Tucker move in slow, fluid circles from where he stood in the center of the corral, following the movement of the mare as it made its way in larger circles around him.

Garrett slid his cell phone from his jeans pocket once again. A quick glance told him there were still no messages from Hannah or the hospital. That had to be a good thing. At least, he prayed it was. If something had happened, surely someone would have contacted him. Hannah had placed his name on the very limited visitor's list, along with his cell phone number.

"You don't need to be here, you know," his brother said, his tone no longer teasing. "Tucker and I can handle things here if you want to go to the hospital to check on Hannah and the baby."

"You and Tucker can't see to the blood draws," Garrett pointed out. "Besides, it's not my place to be there with her," he muttered, despite the pull he felt. The last thing he wanted to do was force himself in her life.

"You're right," Tucker agreed as he turned, following the horse's path. "Best you stay here and be useless, because your focus is anywhere but on what you're supposed to be doing this morning."

"And I'm sure Hannah prefers to be alone in that big old hospital with no one to turn to if she starts feeling overwhelmed with everything," Jackson tossed out. "And with her baby being in neonatal ICU, you can pretty much bet she's at least a little fearful—"

"Point made," Garrett grumbled. If he wasn't already worried about Hannah, he would be hard-pressed not to be after his brothers' guilt-inducing comments. But she'd refused to let him call her father the night before. She'd said she'd needed a little time to let everything sink in, and that even if her father had wanted to come to the hospital to be with them he couldn't. Not while he was sick.

"Someone should be there for her."

"I could go after I'm done here," Tucker volunteered as he relaxed his posture, signaling for the horse circling about him to slow down. "Seeing as how you're digging in your heels at the thought of doing it. I could pick up Autumn on the way. I'm sure she'd like to know how Hannah's doing, her having helped with her baby's birth and all."

Garrett shot his youngest brother an incredulous look. "Appears I'm not the only one lacking focus today. Yours is supposed to be on that horse right now, not on other people's conversations."

Tucker chuckled. "What can I say? The good Lord blessed me with the ability to be a successful multitasker."

"He is, at that," Jackson agreed. "Listen, I'm almost done here. Why don't I run over to the hospital and sit with Hannah for a few hours, seeing as how you and Tucker are going to have your hands full for a while with breaking horses and performing vet duties?"

His brother's suggestion immediately had Garrett rethinking his decision to put off going to the hospital until after he'd done blood draws. There was no reason he couldn't finish them up on the remaining horses later that day, or even tomorrow, for that matter.

"I rescued Hannah and her baby from that rising creek," he said determinedly. "That makes them my responsibility. So, if anyone's going to the hospital to sit with her, it's going to be me. I can see to the blood work later."

Jackson's mouth tugged up at one side, displaying the lone dimple all three brothers had inherited from their father. "Far be it from us to try and usurp your *responsibility*, big brother." He started for the barn, calling back over his shoulder, "Tell Hannah she's in my thoughts."

"Give her my regards as well," Tucker called out as he turned, gaze fixed on the young mare he was working with as he queued her to speed up.

With only a wave of acknowledgment, Garrett walked away. He would go to the hospital, but he was only going to stay long enough to make certain Hannah and the baby were doing all right. He didn't want to feel as if he needed to be there with Hannah and her son. Didn't want to care more than he already did in the brief time since he'd come across Hannah's partially submerged car at the washed-out bridge. Because other than the love he held for his family, he preferred not to care with any real depth for anyone else ever again.

He had just reached his truck when his mother called out to him from the chicken coop, "Garrett!"

Turning, he started toward her, meeting her halfway. "I was just—"

"Heading to the hospital," she finished for him as she switched the basket of eggs she'd collected to the crook of her other arm.

"How did you know?" he asked in surprise.

"Because I know you, and you're not the type of man to leave something unfinished."

He looked at her questioningly.

His mother tilted her head to look up at him, the morning sun glinting off her smiling face. "You're the reason Hannah and her son are alive today, with the good Lord's guiding hand, of course," she was quick to add.

"He's not her son," he said. "She was carrying that little boy for her sister who died in a car accident a few months ago."

"I know," she said, her eyes filled with compassion. "Jackson explained things to me when he called for us to come over and help with the baby's birth. And then Hannah filled in the rest when Autumn and I were helping to deliver her baby. Such a heartbreaking way to become someone's mother. And that's what she is now— that boy's mother. Something Hannah might not have even had the chance to experience if you hadn't come along when you did."

He nodded in agreement.

"That being the case," his mother went on, "it only stands to reason that you would feel the need to look in on them today and for however long they'll be in the hospital. The three of you will forever share a very special connection."

"What if I'd rather not feel any sort of connection to them?" he muttered with a frown.

His mother's expression softened even more. "Honey, I know you'd rather live your life free of any sort of emotional entanglements, but they're a part of life. No matter how large or how small, they help to shape the man you are and the man you will become."

He was content with the man he was now. He had a good life. A supportive family. A successful veterinary business. Part ownership of a thriving rodeo stock company. He didn't need shaping, and he certainly didn't want entanglements of any sort.

"Your needs aside," she said in that motherly tone he knew so well, "you and I both know there are still going to be some hard days ahead for Hannah. Not only with her own physical and emotional recovery, but with the baby's health as well."

"Garrett Austin," he said, recalling Hannah's words the afternoon prior.

His mother looked up at him in confusion. "What?"

"Hannah asked if I would mind if she named her son after me."

His mother's eyes teared up. "What a truly touching thing for her to do."

Ignoring the lump that formed in his throat, Garrett muttered, "I just hope Hannah doesn't regret that decision down the road."

"Whatever makes you think she'll regret it?"

"Because she's been through so much," he explained. "Losing her mother, and then her sister and brother-in-law so close together. Then having to come to terms with the knowledge that she's going to be the one raising her sister's son. And if that wasn't enough for one person to shoulder, she got caught up in a flash flood while in labor. She might have second thoughts on a name she chose when her emotions were so taxed."

His mother nodded. "It's true. That poor dear has had more than her share of tough times. But she's here, her son's here, because of your selfless actions yesterday. You and I both know how easily that ground along the side of the creek could have given way while you sought to rescue Hannah from her car. Garrett, you took such a risk to save them."

He could hear the worry in her voice. "But it didn't. Although I admit I did a fair amount of praying yesterday." The second he'd realized someone was trapped inside that partially submerged car, he knew he would have done whatever he could to help. "From the moment Hannah looked up at me through the driver's side window, her eyes wide with fear, I knew I couldn't—*wouldn't*—let her die. Not like I had Grace."

"Oh, honey," his mother said, her eyes now filled with unshed tears, "your love kept Grace with us longer than she might have been without it. I truly believe that in my heart. But it was her time to go. Just as it's time for you to let go of the guilt you've held on to for so long. Guilt that's not yours to harbor."

His mother became a hazy blur in front of him as moisture gathered in Garrett's eyes. "I don't know if I can."

She reached out and placed a gentle hand atop his forearm. "You'll never know unless you try. And I will say that if Hannah chooses to honor your act of selflessness by naming her son after you, accept it graciously. That little boy couldn't be named after a finer young man."

Garrett cleared the emotion from his throat.

"I am the man I am today because of you and Dad." Leaning forward, he kissed his mother's cheek. "Love you."

"Love you, too."

He drew back. "Don't hold supper on my account if I'm not back in time. I'm not sure how long I'll be staying at the hospital." If Hannah was having a day even half as emotionally trying as the one before, then he would stay and do whatever he could to lift her spirits. Because, like his brother had pointed out, she was all alone.

His mother looked up at him with a tender smile. "Please let Hannah know she and the baby are in our prayers. And, if she needs a place to stay until she's recovered enough to go home, she's more than welcome to stay here at the ranch."

"I'll be sure to let her know," he said and then started back toward his truck.

"Garrett…"

He stopped, casting a glance back at his mother.

"If things get too hard for you, being there at the hospital and all, call me. I'll come relieve you and keep Hannah company."

"I'll be fine," he said determinedly. Because this time it wasn't about him. It was about Hannah and what she needed. That meant pushing past his own emotional hang-ups and proving that he was the man his daddy had raised him to be. With a wave, he strode off, thoughts of Hannah and her precious son front and foremost in his mind.

Hannah paused in the doorway of the hospital's neonatal intensive care unit to cast one more glance back at the incubator that held her sister's precious little son. No, she had to think of him as *her* son now. But guilt kept her from accepting it fully. Austin, as she was calling the child, was Heather's. It didn't seem right claiming him as her own, especially after reminding herself throughout the entire pregnancy that the baby she carried inside her wasn't hers. But her sister and Brian were gone, and their son needed, at the very least, to have a mother in his life. And truth was she needed him, too. So very much.

If not for Garrett Wade, she and Austin would have become yet another flood statistic. Brushing a tear from her cheek, she sent a silent prayer of thanks heavenward. The Lord had sent her a real-life hero if ever there was one. He had come to her rescue not once, not twice, but three times.

First, when he'd pulled her car from the rushing floodwaters and got her to safety. Then when he'd brought his mother and sister-in-law in to help with her baby's untimely arrival during the storm. And then afterward, when the ambulance couldn't get through because the main road remained cut off and the baby had begun having problems breathing. Garrett had gotten them to the hospital—to the medical care her son desperately needed.

"I thought you were supposed to be resting."

As if he'd stepped right out of her thoughts, Hannah turned to find Garrett standing in the hospital corridor, a worried frown on his handsome face. She managed a small smile, even though her heart wasn't in it.

His brow creased as his gaze lit on her face. "Hannah?" Looking past her, he said, the words strained, "The baby?"

"He's holding his own," she answered.

With her reassurance, his focus returned to her. "Thank the Lord."

"I was just going back to my room," she said, feeling drained.

"I'll walk you there."

"Thank you."

Garrett stepped around to place a supportive arm around her waist as he accompanied her. "How are you feeling?"

"I've been better."

He nodded in understanding. "Should you be up moving about on your own?"

"They encourage it," she replied as they made their way down the corridor.

Garrett, bless his heart, didn't look happy about it, but kept his thoughts to himself. "Can I get you anything?" he asked as they turned into her room. "A glass of water? Crackers?"

"No, thank you." She wasn't certain she'd be able to keep anything down.

He turned his back to her as she settled herself into the hospital bed and drew up the covers.

"You can turn around now," she told him.

He did and then stood there looking anything but comfortable.

"You don't have to stay."

He shook his head. "I want to. That is, if you want me to stay."

"I…" The tears she'd been holding back spilled down her cheeks.

"Don't cry," he said with a groan. "I don't have to stay. I probably shouldn't have come." He started for the door.

"Please don't go," she said with a hiccupping sob, futilely trying to brush the tears from her cheeks.

Garrett stopped and then turned, hesitating for a moment before finally making his way over to stand next to her hospital bed. He looked unsure of what to do. Like he wanted to be anywhere else but there, and she couldn't really blame him.

"They're sending me home tomorrow," she explained between tearful gasps.

He exhaled in relief, the worry leaving his face. "So those are happy tears. For a minute there, I thought..." His words trailed off as she began sobbing again. "Hannah?"

"Garrett, I don't have a home to go to," she said. "Not here, anyway."

"Yes, you do," he told her. "Mom wanted me to tell you that you're welcome to stay with them until you're feeling up to traveling back to Colorado."

"That's so kind of her," she said, her voice cracking with emotion. "But how can I even think about leaving Austin? That's what I'm going to call him, even though his given name will be Garrett Austin Sanders."

"I like it," he told her. "But then I'm a bit partial to the first two names, having had it myself for the past thirty-four years. And, just to be clear, the invitation from my mom was for the both of you. She's raised three sons of her own. She'll be more than happy to help you with the baby."

"That's just it," she said with a sob. "They want to send me home without him. Because he came early, he's not ready to leave the hospital yet."

"Then you should stay here with him."

"I already asked, but there aren't enough available beds for me to continue staying on here." She looked up, meeting his gaze, her heart breaking. "Garrett, I can't leave my baby here all alone. Not while he's hooked up to all those machines."

He placed his hand over hers, giving it a comforting squeeze. "He's in good hands, Hannah. You need to focus on that. Did they say how long until he can go home?"

She shook her head. "It's too soon to know, but it could be weeks."

"Whatever it takes to get your son strong enough to come home to you," he told her, his determined words touching Hannah deeply. "In the meantime, I'll bring you to the hospital anytime you want and pick you up whenever you're ready to come home. I'll even stay when I can."

"Garrett, I can't ask that of you," she said, shaking her head in refusal.

"You didn't," he said with a warm smile. "I offered."

"But your job…"

"Isn't going to be an issue," he assured her. "Most of my income comes from my share of the rodeo stock contracting business I co-own with my brothers, and we aren't into the start of the rodeo season yet, so there is no issue there. As for my being a vet, I work mostly with our horses, but make a few large animal calls here and there. We have another vet in town who can cover for me if the situation arises."

Her fingers curled around his hand. "You are such a good man, Garrett Wade. I'm so thankful God brought you into my life." She thought about the precious little boy she'd given birth to and added with a teary smile, "Our lives."

Before he could respond, her cell phone, which was lying atop the wheeled side table, rang out. With his free hand, his other still held in Hannah's determined grasp, Garrett reached for the phone and handed it over to her.

"It's my father," she said with a worried frown. "What do I tell him?"

"Probably best to start with the truth," he answered. "He's bound to pick up on your emotional state and will worry more if he thinks you're keeping something from him."

She nodded. Garrett was right. She needed to tell her father what had happened. Bringing the phone to her ear, she answered, "Hi, Dad."

Garrett mouthed, "I'll step out and give you some privacy."

She shook her head, praying he would stay. His being there gave her comfort and helped to calm her fears.

Thankfully, Garrett nodded, falling silent as she took the call.

"Hi, Dad."

"Hi, honey," her father replied and then paused to cough, the sound clearly coming from deep in his chest.

She gasped. "Dad, you sound terrible. Have you seen your doctor yet?"

"Not yet," he admitted. "I was hoping the cough would start to ease up now that the cold's finally out of my head, but it hasn't. I'm going to call Dr. Mason today."

"I'm glad." She had enough worries on her plate without adding her father's ailing health to them.

"I wasn't calling to talk about me. I was worried about you," he said. "I thought you were supposed to get home last night, but when I woke up this morning and realized you hadn't made it home... Well, all sorts of things went through my mind."

"I'm sorry to have caused you worry, Dad," she said. "I never meant to. I really thought I'd be home last night."

"It's all right, honey. All that matters is that you're all right," he said, unable to keep the emotion from his voice. "I know how hard it had to be for you to take your sister's and Brian's ashes to Shoshone Falls. I wish you would have let me ride along with you."

Having lost both his wife and his daughter

in just over a year's time, the task of delivering Heather's ashes to a place that was very special to her would have been unbearably hard on him. Especially with him not feeling up to par. "You weren't feeling well, and taking Heather and Brian's ashes to the falls was really something I needed to do on my own." In truth, the long drive had given her time to reflect, to mourn, to start to plan her future. One that now included raising a child.

"I understand," he said. "When do you think you'll get here?"

"About that…" she began.

"Hannah," he said worriedly. "What's wrong?" The question was followed by another round of coughing.

This was something she would rather have told her father in person, so he could see that she and the baby were all right. But that wasn't an option. Not with her son needing to remain in NICU for an undetermined amount of time. "I'm in the hospital."

"Dear Lord," he groaned.

"I'm fine, Dad," she hurried to assure him. "But I was in labor when Garrett rescued me."

"Rescued?" her father gasped between coughs.

Hannah cringed. Why had she even brought that part up? Her father hadn't needed to know about that. "Dad? Are you okay?"

"I've been better," he rasped out as his coughing subsided. "Hannah, what happened? Where are you?"

She went on to explain everything that had happened in a shortened version and with far less detail to spare her father any further stress.

"Well, thank the good Lord for sending that young man there. I couldn't bear to lose you, too."

"You won't."

"How is the baby?" he asked hesitantly, as if fearing what her answer might be. "I know my grandson wasn't due to arrive for another month or so."

"Apparently, your grandson was tired of waiting. Garrett Austin came into the world wailing loudly." And he had, but that was before her son's breathing issues began.

"You named him after the man who rescued you from the flood," he acknowledged, his words filled with emotion.

"Yes," she answered. "If not for Garrett, we wouldn't be here today." She felt Garrett tense up beside her. Her praise might embarrass him, but it was true all the same. "Your grandson is small, and in need of a little extra care, but he's going to be fine," she said determinedly. He had to be. Like her father, she didn't think she could bear the loss of yet another person she held dear.

"That explains why you didn't call."

"I was waiting to talk to the doctor this morning before I called you. He came by a little while ago to tell me that they're releasing me tomorrow, but Austin has to remain in the neonatal intensive care unit until he's strong enough to go home. Do you mind watching the boys until I can get home?"

"You don't even have to ask," he answered with a wheeze. "But I'd prefer to be there with you and the baby."

Her frown deepened. "Dad, listen to you. You sound awful. As much as I would love to have you here with us, I have to ask you not to come. It's too risky for the baby. And if I get sick, I won't be able to be around him either."

"Ah, honey, I understand. I just hate the thought of the two of you being there all alone."

She looked up at Garrett and managed a small smile. "We won't be alone. We have Garrett and his family here to watch over us. Mrs. Wade has even offered her home to me during my stay here. So, please, go call your doctor and get yourself well, so you can love up your grandson when the time comes for me to bring him home."

"I will," he said with a resigned sigh. "Make sure you keep me updated with how things are going. You and my grandson are all I have left in this world, and as soon as the doctor considers me well enough to be around the two of you, and I can find someone to watch over the dogs, I'll be there."

"You're all we have," she replied. "So please take care of yourself."

"You can count on it. And tell that young man who rescued you that I look forward to meeting him someday soon. I want to thank him in person for what he's done for you and my grandson."

"I'll let him know. I love you, Dad."

"I love you, too, honey."

Hannah hung up and looked to Garrett. "He sounds awful."

"A cold?" Garrett surmised.

"Yes," she said with a worried frown. "It's pretty deep in his chest, but he assured me he's going to get in to see his doctor."

"Then you need to set that worry aside and focus on getting your strength back, and on that little one of yours, so we can get him home with his big brothers as soon as possible."

"Brothers?" she repeated in confusion.

He looked chagrined. "I wasn't trying to listen in, but I heard you ask your father if he'd mind watching over your boys for a little while longer. I know how hard being away from your boys for any length of time is going to be for you."

She smiled. "Oh, it will be."

He studied her, as if trying to find the humor in the situation. "I'm sure Mom wouldn't have a problem with them coming here to stay with you until you can go back to Steamboat Springs. Unless they're in school. I have no idea how old your boys are."

"Garrett, you're sweet to think of my boys, but you should know that Buddy and Bandit already graduated from school."

His chestnut brows lifted.

"Puppy school," she added with a grin. "They're my two-year-old golden retrievers."

He let out a husky chuckle. "You had me worried for a moment. I was wondering what mother would ever think to name her son Bandit."

"He likes to take things and hide them," she explained, the temporary redirection of her thoughts to something other than the seriousness going on in her life helped to lighten her heavy heart. Hannah sighed. "I'm really going to miss having those two underfoot."

Garrett squeezed her hand. "It won't be for long. We'll have you home with all three of your *boys* before you know it."

The conviction in his words made her believe that no matter what the coming weeks brought about everything would be okay. Garrett would make certain of that. Hannah sent up a silent prayer of thanks to the Lord for sending her this unexpected pillar of strength in the form of this kind, lone-dimpled cowboy.

Chapter Four

Garrett glanced again at the clock on the kitchen wall. It was five minutes past the last time he'd looked. It had been five minutes the time before that. He should have taken his mother up on her offer to pick Hannah up from the hospital that morning and bring her home. He hadn't. And, for the life of him, he couldn't say why.

Every trip he made to that place stirred up memories. At first, they were of Grace and those final days he'd had her in his life. But then other memories took over. Memories of the storm. Of Hannah's pretty, fear-stricken face looking up at him from where she sat trapped in her car. Of the trust he'd seen in her eyes when he'd told her she was going to be all right. Of her brave smile.

Frowning, Garrett shook his head and crossed the room to grab his cowboy hat from the end table, settling it onto his head. Guilt pricked at his conscience. How could he allow his memories of the only woman he'd ever loved—girl, actually, because that's what Grace had been when she'd died—to be so easily set aside?

Not that he hadn't gone out a time or two during his rodeo days. But he'd done so, knowing those women were more interested in snagging themselves a professional rodeo rider than in dating the man he was inside. They'd been safe, because he knew feelings would never come into play. When he would tell them he wasn't interested in starting a real relationship, they would simply move on to another. But Hannah, in what little time he had known her, had made him feel so many things—fear at the thought of her or the baby she'd been carrying dying, determination to save her like he hadn't been able to with Grace, the need to protect her and admiration for the strength he saw inside of her.

His cell phone rang, pulling Garrett from his troubled thoughts. He hurried to dig it out of his jeans pocket, praying, as he did every time his phone rang, that it wasn't the hospital calling to say he needed to get there right away. Only in Grace's case, it had been her father who had made the call, telling Garrett to get to the hospital right away. His trepidation eased when he saw the caller ID on the screen.

"Justin."

"Garrett," his friend said in greeting.

"How's the new foal getting along?" Thankfully, it had survived what sounded like a rough delivery. One Justin had tended to on his own, thanks to the poorly-timed storm.

"Couldn't be better," the sheriff replied. "The reason I was calling was to let you know where Miss Sanders's car was towed to, and to let you know that they found a small overnight bag in the backseat. I picked it up and was going to run it over to her, but I wasn't sure if she was still in the hospital, or if she had already been released. I know they don't keep anyone in for long these days."

"I was just about to leave for the hospital. Hannah's being released today. Are you at the office?"

"For another hour or so."

"I'll swing by and pick the bag up on my way to the hospital. Hannah might want to wear something else to come home in." At least, this way she would have a choice. His mother had taken the clothes Hannah wore the day before when she'd gone to visit her and the baby at the hospital and had washed them for her so she would have something clean to wear when she was released. They were already in his truck, all neatly folded inside of a canvas tote.

"How's the baby?"

"Unfortunately, he's not able to come home yet," Garrett replied with a frown, hating that Hannah had to be separated from her son. "But it won't be long. She'll be staying at my parents' place until her son is able to travel back to Colorado with her."

"I didn't realize she was so far from home," Justin said. "I need to fill out a report, but I can do that once she gets settled in at the ranch. In the meantime, I'll be sure to keep her and the baby in my prayers."

"I'm sure Hannah would appreciate that. See you soon." After hanging up the phone, Garrett grabbed his truck keys and headed out.

He stopped in the building he'd constructed next to his house that served as both a clinic and supply storage to double-check his schedule before setting out. Thankfully, he only had a few appointments scheduled for the next week or so, vaccination updates and such, since he'd be making a fair number of trips to the hospital with Hannah to see her son.

Her son. That tiny little blessing Garrett had held in his arms; perhaps he would have had his own son if Grace had lived to give him the family they'd talked about having someday. Who would have thought a baby could have such a pull on a man's heart? But Hannah's son had done just that.

Lord, please keep that precious little baby safe, he prayed and then headed for his truck.

Fifteen minutes later, Garrett pulled into a parking space outside of the sheriff's office. He stepped from his truck just as the building's front door swung open and Justin, dressed in his uniform, came out to greet him, a quilted floral travel bag held in one hand.

"Cute bag," Garrett remarked with a grin, as he moved toward his friend. "The pink roses go remarkably well with your uniform."

Justin held it up, turning it to and fro. "Thanks. I thought so, too." He handed the bag over to Garrett, and then extended his hand, giving Garrett's a firm shake. "How are you holding up?"

"Me?"

Justin nodded. "You. It's no secret that you've had an eventful few days. Flood rescue, baby delivery and then personally taking on the responsibility of looking in on Miss Sanders and her little boy."

"I see you've been talking to Jackson," Garrett said.

"Your father, actually," the sheriff admitted. "I ran into him this morning at Abby's. He snagged the last crème-filled donut, leaving me with the remaining selection of cake donuts."

"Not surprised," Garrett replied with a chuckle. All the Wade men had a sweet tooth.

"He was on his way out, so we didn't have much of a chance to talk, but he did tell me that you were spending a lot of time at the hospital with Miss Sanders." His expression sobered somewhat. "I know that can't be easy for you."

He nodded. As Jackson's best friend, Justin had been around when Grace took ill. He knew what Garrett had been through. "It hasn't," he answered honestly. "But Hannah's father is sick and can't be here with her."

"What about her mother?"

"Passed away. And then her sister died a few months ago. And being miles from home doesn't make things any easier."

Justin's teasing grin flattened. "And now she's going through all this." He shook his head. "The Lord knew what He was doing when He placed her in your family's lives."

Before Garrett could reply, one of the deputies came out to let Justin know that his sister was on the line and that she sounded upset. Excusing himself, he immediately went to take the call.

Garrett understood the look of concern he'd seen on his friend's face as he'd strode off. A little over a year earlier, Lainie, Justin's little sister, lost her husband when a drunk driver struck their car. She and her seven-year-old son had remained in Sacramento, despite the urgings of Justin and his parents for her to move back home.

Though he'd never made mention of his suspicions to anyone, Garrett thought that at least part of the reason Lainie hadn't come home was because of Jackson. While she and Jackson never dated, there had been a time when Garrett thought his younger brother might have feelings for Lainie and her for him. But then Jackson went off to ride in the rodeo and Lainie headed to college, finding love elsewhere. Now, with no husband to take care of her and her son, Justin was determined to be there for them. Just as Garrett would be there for Hannah and hers. For now.

"Morning," the two nurses on duty in the NICU said in quiet greeting when Hannah stepped into the room.

"Morning," she replied, keeping her voice low as well. Only Austin and one other newborn, a little girl born two months too soon, were being cared for in the neonatal intensive care unit at that time. Seeing that fragile little girl, so much smaller than her own son, made Hannah want to cry. Life could be so unfair sometimes.

She had taken only two steps across the room, in the direction of the incubator that held her newborn son, when she noticed an odd glow filling Austin's temporary crib. A sense of unease filled her as she hurried over to it. Inside, her son, dressed in only a diaper, his eyes covered with a small white mask, was bathed in the glow of a deep blue light.

With a worried gasp, Hannah pressed a hand to the clear side of the incubator.

"It's called a bili light," a soft voice from behind her stated.

Hannah glanced back to find the younger of the two NICU nurses, Jessica, if she remembered correctly, standing there, an empathetic smile on her face. "What is a bili light?" she asked anxiously, her attention returning to her son.

"A type of phototherapy used when a newborn is jaundiced," she explained.

"Why is he jaundiced?" Hannah asked, her panic growing. Why hadn't she read up on more than just what could happen during pregnancy? Maybe because what happened after were the things her sister should have known about. Not her. And when Heather and Brian had died, her focus had been on getting through the grief.

"Jaundice occurs when a baby's blood has more bilirubin than it can get rid of," the young nurse said calmly.

"Is it serious?" Hannah asked, her heart pounding.

"It can be," she answered honestly. "But not in

most cases. This type of jaundice is quite common in newborns because their organs aren't able to get rid of the excess bilirubin very well, giving them a tinge of yellow to their skin coloring and to the whites of their eyes. The lights you see above your son are able to pass through an infant's skin and break down the bilirubin into a form that the baby can eliminate. That's why we have him lying there in only his diaper. To expose as much of his skin as possible."

"How long will he have to be under these lights?" Hannah asked, trying not to let her fear show.

"Typically, twenty-four to forty-eight hours. At that point, the newborn's liver can usually handle the bilirubin itself."

"And if it can't?" she heard herself asking, unsure if she really wanted to know the answer.

"Depending on the severity of the jaundice, the infant could require a blood transfusion. Sometimes, they just need more time under the lights and plenty of hydration." She moved to stand next to Hannah. "But your little one's case isn't severe. So try not to worry."

If only it were that easy, she thought with a frown. "I'm his mother," Hannah said, still mentally trying to come to terms with that fact. "It's my job to worry over him. Wouldn't you if you had a child hooked up to all these wires and tubes, and now *this*?"

Jessica nodded. "I would, and I did."

"You did?" Hannah repeated.

"I know firsthand what you're going through," the young nurse answered, her gaze settling on Hannah's son. "My son was born six weeks early. There were complications with my delivery and I nearly lost Dustin. But my son is a fighter, thank the Lord, and stubbornly clung to life while being hooked up to all of these tubes and wires. Just as your son is now," she noted. "He struggled to breathe. His body couldn't regulate its temperature. Like Austin, he was jaundiced and had to lay for days under the bili lights." She looked to Hannah. "Today my son is a healthy, happy seven-year-old."

"Thank you for sharing that with me," Hannah said with a grateful smile. Knowing that Jessica had gone through what she was going through now, and that her son had grown into a healthy little boy, helped to calm her fears.

"I wanted you to know that I truly do understand what you're going through right now, beyond the knowledge I've gained as a medical professional. In fact, my son is the reason I decided to get my GED and then pursue a degree in nursing, my focus on neonatal care."

That meant Jessica hadn't graduated from

high school. She had to assume it was because of the baby, because she didn't look to be much more than twenty-five and she'd said that her little boy was seven. It was so hard to think of children having children, but Jessica had made something of her life for the sake of her son. Her story was a reminder to Hannah that she wasn't alone when it came to surviving life's hardships.

"I'm so glad things turned out the way they did for you," Hannah said with a soft smile.

"If they hadn't, I would have spent the rest of my life blaming myself for it," Jessica admitted as she reached into the incubator to check Austin's vitals. "When I found out I was expecting, I spent months in denial when I should have been having prenatal visits and taking vitamins, and putting my baby's needs first."

"You were young," Hannah said sympathetically. "I'm twenty-seven, and discovering that I was going to be someone's mother was more than a little overwhelming for me. It's something you know is destined to change your life forever."

Jessica nodded in agreement as she adjusted the position of Hannah's sleeping son. "More than I ever imagined. However, I wasn't as blessed as you. Dustin's father wanted nothing to do with us, unlike your son's."

Her son's father? She had to be referring to

Garrett. There had been no one else there for her. The memory of seeing Austin cradled ever so tenderly in those big, strong arms came rushing back. Watching the cowboy's worried expression fade away, to be replaced by one of awe and wonder, had touched her deeply.

"Garrett isn't Austin's father," Hannah explained, and then added sadly, "His father is dead. He and my sister, Heather—Austin's biological parents—were killed in a car accident a few months ago. I had offered to be a surrogate mother for them, because Heather couldn't carry a baby to term."

Jessica's expression changed instantly. "I'm so sorry. I just assumed…"

"Please, don't apologize," Hannah said. "I can see where you might have gotten that impression, seeing as how Garrett brought me to the hospital and has been here with me every day since I was admitted. But he and I only met a few days ago."

Surprise flashed across Jessica's face.

Hannah went on, "Garrett rescued me from a flash flood I got caught up in while driving through Bent Creek, after which I went into full labor. If not for him, my son and I might not be here today."

"That had to be so frightening," Jessica said,

a hand pressed to her chest. "I'm so glad he was able to reach you in time."

"My prayers were definitely answered that day," she said.

"Morning," the other nurse said from a small desk near the doorway.

"Good morning," a familiar male voice replied, immediately drawing Hannah's gaze.

With a warm smile aimed in her direction, Garrett crossed the room to where Hannah stood with Jessica.

"Morning," Hannah greeted, surprised by how happy she was to see him. Maybe it was seeing a somewhat familiar face when she was feeling so alone. All she knew was that Garrett's presence seemed to wrap around her like a security blanket, instantly soothing some of her growing fears. Realizing she was still staring up at him, she turned her attention back to her son, who looked so incredibly small and fragile inside the lamp-lit glass enclosure.

"I need to go update your son's records," Jessica told her. "I'll be back in a little bit to look in on him."

Garrett moved to stand beside her when Jessica walked away. "How are you holding up?"

"Not well, I'm afraid," she admitted, wrapping her arms about herself. "I don't know how I'm supposed to leave him."

"I know it won't be easy," he said, his tone filled with compassion, "but he's got to stay here and grow strong. You'll see him every day until he's ready to come home with you."

She nodded. "I know." But the thought of leaving Austin tore at her heart.

"We don't have to leave just yet," he told her. "I don't have anything I need to be doing today."

Hannah fought the sudden sting of unshed tears. "If it's all right with you, I'd like to stay for a little while longer. Austin's had a setback."

With a worried frown, Garrett looked down into the incubator. "What's happened?"

"He's jaundiced," she answered. "That's why they have him under these special lights."

He gave a nod of understanding. "It's not uncommon for a newborn, especially one that was born prematurely, to have issues with jaundice."

Hannah sniffled softly, fighting to hold back the tears. "A mother is supposed to be able to make everything all right. Because that's what I am now, aren't I? His mother? But my son is so tiny and helpless, and there's nothing I can do to help him."

His hand moved to wrap around hers. "You are his mother, Hannah. And you need to stay strong for him. Don't let your fears push your faith aside. Trust in the Lord to heal Austin and give him the strength he needs."

"I'm trying, Garrett," she said with a soft sob, clinging tightly to the hand holding hers, as if doing so would help give her the strength she would need to get through this. "But sometimes it gets so overwhelming, and I feel so alone."

"I know," he said, giving her hand a sympathetic squeeze. "But you're not alone, Hannah. You have me, and you have my family here to support you while you are going through this. We'll weather this rough patch together. I promise."

She was not alone. Garrett hadn't abandoned her. A woman he didn't even know, had no obligation to. No, he'd come back to check on them. Offering her comfort and support. He was a good man. The kind a woman dreamed of coming into her life someday. Only, her life was far too complicated now, and that "someday" had been pushed aside by the need to focus solely on the baby she would be raising on her own.

When Garrett's hand left hers, Hannah found herself wishing he hadn't pulled away. His gentle touch was comforting, giving her a strength she couldn't seem to find on her own right now.

"Have you eaten?" he asked.

"They brought a breakfast tray to my room this morning."

"But did you eat?" he pressed.

Hannah shook her head. "No. I wasn't hungry."

"I figured as much," he replied. "Hannah, you need to eat to keep your strength up, or you won't be any good to your son. Tell you what, how about you and I take a walk down to the cafeteria?"

"He's right," Jessica said, joining them once more alongside the incubator. Reaching inside, she shifted Austin slightly. "You need to keep your strength up. Trust me, I know. Go on and get yourself something to eat. I'll be here to watch over your son for you."

She had no doubt that her son would be in capable hands, but it was still hard to walk away. But Garrett and Jessica were right. She needed to keep up her strength. For Austin's sake, if not her own. "Thank you," Hannah said. "We won't be long."

"We'll be here," Jessica replied with a smile as she cast a glance toward Hannah's son.

Garrett escorted Hannah from the room, a supportive hand placed at the small of her back as they made their way down the corridor. "Should I get you a wheelchair? It's a bit of a walk to the hospital's cafeteria."

She glanced over at him with a grateful smile. "I don't think that will be necessary. As I said yesterday, they prefer me to be up and moving about. Even if a bit more slowly than my normal pace."

"I'm sorry," he replied with a frown. "I do remember you mentioning that. Truth is, I don't have much experience with this kind of thing. There's a big difference between a horse and you giving birth."

Much to her surprise, a soft giggle pushed past her lips. "I would hope so."

Color flooded his tanned cheeks. "That didn't exactly come out the way I meant it to. What I was trying to say was—"

"You don't need to explain yourself," Hannah said, cutting him off. "This is all new to me, too."

They stopped at the elevator doors and Garrett reached out to push the down button. "Fortunately, my mother has a lot of experience with having babies. She'll be able to help you navigate this new part of your life. Even Autumn will be able to answer a lot of your questions. She helped with the raising of Blue for most of her young life."

The elevator doors slid open and they stepped inside. "Blue?"

"My niece," he answered as the doors closed. He jabbed at the floor button that would take them to the cafeteria. "Tucker eloped with Autumn's sister back when he was riding the rodeo circuit. But they were young, and things didn't work out the way he thought they would. In fact,

Summer walked out on him without even a note of explanation, and it wasn't until just recently that he learned of his daughter's existence, when Autumn came to tell him of her sister's passing. Blue's five now."

"She kept his daughter from him all those years?" she said, her heart going out to Garrett's brother.

"Summer had her reasons for doing what she did," he said. "Not that I agree with them, but then, I didn't grow up in a broken family the way she had. My brothers and I were raised with the love of both parents, who are still happily married today."

"I can't even imagine what it would have been like to grow up without two loving parents." Like her son would have to do, she thought sadly. But she would do everything in her power to make certain he always felt loved. Something else struck her at that moment. Looking to Garrett, she said, "So your brother married his wife's sister?"

"Her twin sister," he answered as the elevator arrived at their floor. "While they grew up together down in Braxton, Texas, Autumn and Summer are, or I suppose that should be *were*, two very different personalities. Autumn is a better fit for the man my brother has grown into.

And she loves his daughter, her niece, as if Blue were her very own."

Just as I will love my nephew, Hannah thought to herself. He would never doubt her. She'd make certain of that.

Garrett's worried gaze slid over to Hannah who was seated in the passenger seat of his truck. "You doing okay?"

She hesitated before nodding her reply. "A little tired. That's all."

"I think that's to be expected," he assured her, his attention returning to the road ahead. "You've been through a lot these past few days. And hospital beds aren't known for inducing the most restful night's sleep."

"To be honest, I am looking forward to spending the night in a real bed again," Hannah said, looking out the passenger side window. "I just wish…"

"That Austin were here with you," Garrett finished for her, his tone gentle.

"Yes," she replied with a heart-wrenching sigh.

"It won't be long," he said. "And I'll take you back to see your son after supper." The hospital was in the next town over, so the drive wasn't overly long. Twenty-five minutes at the most.

"I've taken you away from your responsibilities enough for one day," she said, looking his way.

"Right now, you're my responsibility," he said, wondering the second the words left his mouth where they had come from. While he had every intention of helping Hannah out while she was there, a position he had set his mind never to put himself in again after losing Grace, he would do so without any sort of emotional commitment. Cut and dry was how he preferred things when it came to his emotions. It was safer that way.

"As soon as I can arrange it, I'm going to have a rental car delivered. That will allow me to travel to and from the hospital without having to impose on you or your family."

A frown tugged at his mouth. "Are you sure that's a good idea? Driving so soon after giving birth? I know I'm a vet, but I would think your body would need a little healing time before doing so." Steering a car used abdominal muscles which had to be weakened from carrying a baby. Not to mention all the physical strain a body went through giving birth.

Her lips pressed together.

"Hannah?"

"It might be a little sooner than the doctor suggested," she confessed, avoiding his gaze.

"I thought as much," he replied with a sigh. "Look, I know you don't want to have to depend on others to help you with things you've always been able to do on your own. But this isn't a normal situation. Your car was totaled in a flood. You went into labor sooner than expected. Your son requires additional medical care. Your father is sick and unable to help you out right now. Let my family help you through this. Let *me* help you."

Garrett couldn't take the words back. He wanted to help Hannah. It was the Christian thing to do. And there was no risk of getting emotionally caught up in the situation as he had with Grace. His heart would have to do more than beat for that to happen, but the organ had been numb for pretty much half his life.

"You're a stubborn man, Garrett Wade," Hannah told him with a small smile.

"Determined," he countered with a grin.

She sighed softly. "I suppose there will be plenty of time to practice being self-sufficient once Austin and I go home. And you needn't worry about us financially. My insurance will cover most of our care, and, besides the money I have put away in my savings, we have the life insurance Heather and Brian left to me, along with the sale of their house."

"What if your insurance doesn't cover Austin's care?" he asked.

"It will," she assured him. "With no surrogacy contract between my sister and her husband and myself, something we felt no need to have, and with their passing, I can legally claim him as my own."

"And what about your sister's husband's family? Do you think they'll try and fight you on this?"

She shook her head. "Brian didn't have the best home life growing up and hadn't been in contact with his family since leaving home at seventeen. Heather and Brian had made their wishes clear to me, that if anything were ever to happen to them they wanted me to take over the raising of their child, or children, if the Lord saw fit to bless them with more than one."

"You might not need help financially, but you might find yourself in need of other forms of assistance while you're here. So, until you're able to go home to Colorado, consider yourself tucked securely beneath the Wade family wing."

Moisture filled her eyes. "Thank you."

He looked away, not wanting to see the tears pooling in her eyes. Hannah's tears had a way of getting to him, making him feel things he'd just as soon not feel. Like connected and vulnerable and protective, all at the same time. "You're welcome."

Silence fell between them for several minutes. Hannah's attention was fixed on the land that stretched out around them. His family's land. While Garrett struggled to focus on anything but the woman beside him. He'd never felt so distracted.

"That's my place," he announced as they drove past the barn-style ranch house that sat off in the distance. "The smaller building next to the house is my vet clinic, not that it gets used too often. Most of my work is done on-site, rather than having my customers transport their cows and horses."

"I love how the house, barn and your vet building are all the same shade of red trimmed in white."

"Chili pepper," he said. "At least, that's what the builder said the shade was called when I chose it from the color strips he gave me to look over. The white was listed as marshmallow. Not sure when paint selections became centered around food, but I'd rather go back to having it referred to as just plain red or basic white. No way was I going to tell my brothers I had decided to trim my house in marshmallow. Takes the cowboy right out of a man."

Hannah laughed, the sound beyond sweet to Garrett's ears. "I think you still have plenty of cowboy left in you."

He chuckled. "Appreciate that. Sorry to have

rambled on about house paint of all things. I'm not the best conversationalist. Truth is, most of my time is spent with animals."

Her sweet smile widened. "I think you converse quite well. And I'm grateful for any conversation that helps keep my thoughts from straying to things I have no control over."

He was glad to hear her say that. He'd been trying to do just that, knowing how upset she'd been when they'd left the hospital that afternoon. After another mile or so, Garrett pointed off to the side. "That's Tucker's place." A one-story log house with a sprawling cottonwood shading a section of the front yard. Garrett smiled as his gaze passed over the swing he and Jackson had hung from one of the thick cottonwood branches when Blue had first come to Bent Creek. Their niece had spent countless hours on that swing, much to Tucker and Autumn's dismay, as they'd been the ones who'd had to stand there, pushing her for hours on end.

"Jackson's place, which I took you to during the storm, is a few miles down the road, just before the bridge. Or, at least, what used to be the bridge," he corrected.

"Do many people use that bridge?" Hannah asked.

"A few, but it's mostly my family, since the

road cuts through our ranch," he told her. "We've all built our homes along this road."

"I'm sorry you lost your quickest access to town."

He shrugged. "Not a big deal. The bridge has been washed out a couple of times before. We're used to it. We'll just have to allow ourselves extra time to get to town, since we'll have to take the long way in until they get a new bridge up in its place."

"It's nice that you all live close by each other," Hannah said with a sad smile. "Heather and Brian lived on the outskirts of Steamboat Springs, so we were able to see each other often. I'm thankful now for the time we were able to spend together."

"I never really gave it any thought," he admitted. "It's all I've ever known, where they're concerned. We grew up together, rode in the rodeo together, at least for a while, work together, and live on the same stretch of land. I suppose we just take being together for granted." Something he should have known better than to do. Mari, his baby sister, had been taken from them far too soon after she'd contracted meningitis. Only six years old. And then his high school sweetheart, who had been on the verge of adulthood. Even Summer had died far too young.

"Life has no guarantees," Hannah said with a frown.

Garrett nodded solemnly. "That I know."

"You've lost someone close to you?"

His gaze pinned to the road, he replied, "Haven't we all?" Needing to redirect their conversation to something that touched less upon his own painful past, he nodded in the direction they were traveling. "The Triple W is about a half mile down the road."

"The Triple W?"

"The Triple W Rodeo Ranch," he clarified. "It's the property my brothers and I grew up on. My parents still live there, while my brothers and I have built our own houses elsewhere. The main ranch is where we keep the livestock trailers, supplies for the rodeo as well as feed and medical supplies. It has the largest barn and several smaller areas of fenced-off land that allow us to keep the horses we will be taking to upcoming rodeos in a more contained area. Saves us from chasing them all over creation."

She looked to him questioningly. "Shouldn't that be the Four W Rodeo Ranch? You, your brothers and your father."

If he and his brothers had gotten their way, it would have been. But their father preferred to remain in the background, helping when needed, but not actually being a part of their growing business.

"When Dad retired from the rodeo, he spent years building this place into one of the most respected horse ranches around. People knew they could be assured of purchasing quality horses from the Big W Horse Ranch. So, by the time the three of us boys were grown and done riding the rodeo circuit, he was more than ready to take a step back from the business, turning everything over to us. We began taking in, as well as breeding our own, horses for rodeo competition."

"I never really gave any thought to where rodeos get their livestock from," she said. "I've never even been to one."

"You haven't?" he said in surprise. It was hard to remember that going to rodeos wasn't just the norm for some families. But it was all he had known.

Hannah shook her head. "No. I was more the stay-at-home, bookworm type."

He took a moment to study her before glancing back at the road. "Bookworm type, huh? Not sure I see it."

She arched a questioning brow. "Why is that? Because I'm not holding a book?"

He shrugged. "Maybe because you were traveling all alone, even when you were so far along in your pregnancy. Throw in your braving a raging flood, and I see you much more as an adventurer."

Her smile withered away, making Garrett wonder what he'd said wrong. "I didn't set out seeking adventure. I drove to Shoshone Falls in Idaho to spread my sister's and her husband's ashes in a place that held special meaning for them. And I was only alone because Dad was feeling under the weather. Not that I minded making the drive by myself. It gave me time to work on coming to terms with things."

"I'm sorry you had to do that," he said regretfully, wishing he hadn't taken the conversation in that direction. No matter how unintentional it had been.

"It was hard," she admitted. "But doing that for my sister gave me a sense of peace that I had been struggling to find. Partly because I was seeing my sister's wishes carried through, but some of that peace came from the untouched beauty of mountains and prairies that surrounded me during my drive to Shoshone Falls." She glanced around. "I would imagine that living here, surrounded by such a picturesque view of nature, offers the same kind of inner peace."

He'd never thought of it that way, but after Grace had died he'd spent hours each day riding across the ranch, stopping at times to just sit and take in the view. He hadn't thought so at the time, because the pain had been too great, but looking back he supposed he had found some sort of solace back then as he'd sat looking out over God's land.

"It does," he answered with a nod as he turned into the drive leading up to his parents' house.

Garrett's mother stepped out onto the porch, waving as she welcomed them home. Autumn followed, smiling warmly, and Blue came hurrying out behind them, her long, chestnut curls bouncing wildly around her tiny shoulders.

"Looks like you have a 'welcome home' committee awaiting you," he said, casting a look in Hannah's direction. "Should I apologize now? My family can be somewhat overwhelming at times."

Her expression softened, and tears immediately filled her eyes.

"Hannah?" Garrett said worriedly.

"That's so kind of them," she said with a sniffle.

Relief swept through him with her response. She wasn't upset. She was touched. "Prepare to be smothered by kindness," he warned with a grin as he came to a stop in the drive.

Chapter Five

"Hello," Hannah said, feeling slightly anxious as she and Garrett stepped up onto his mother's porch, the overnight bag he'd managed to salvage from her flood-totaled car clutched in his large, sun-browned hand.

"Welcome to our home," his mother greeted with a warm smile.

"Thank you for having me," she replied.

"Don't be too grateful," Garrett said with a charming grin. "She might never let you leave. Mom loves to coddle people."

Garrett's sister-in-law, Autumn, laughed. "He's right. In fact, her homemade cookies, of which I've eaten plenty of since coming here, are one of the reasons I stayed."

"Me, too!" the little girl Hannah presumed to be Tucker's daughter chimed in.

"Tucker and my granddaughter being the biggest reasons Autumn decided to stick around," his mother said with a knowing smile.

Blue nodded. "Daddy, too. He loves Grandma's cookies."

They all laughed.

"I meant that your aunt Autumn stayed not only because of my cookies, but because she fell in love with your daddy."

The little girl's head swung around, her gaze lifting to Hannah's face. "If Grandma gives you cookies, will you fall in love with my uncle Garrett? He has to live in his house all by himself."

Hannah tried not to smile overly big at his niece's innocent query. It was clear she loved her uncle and worried about him being lonely. Before she could respond, Garrett answered for her.

"Cookies can't make two people fall in love," he gently explained.

"I beg to differ," his mother replied. "My oatmeal raisin cookies won your father's heart over."

Blue giggled.

"You had his heart from the first day he met you," Garrett promptly reminded her.

"I had his attention," his mother corrected. "But it was my oatmeal raisin cookies that convinced your father that his heart was indeed on the right track."

"I can see that there is no use trying to set

Blue straight on her cookies-and-love misconception." He turned to his niece. "Miss Sanders will be going back to where her family lives in Steamboat Springs when her baby is big enough to travel. So, cookies or not, she isn't going to be sticking around for long." He turned to Hannah. "If you haven't guessed already, this adorable little chatterbox is my niece, Blue Belle Wade."

"What a pretty name," Hannah said.

"My mommy named me after a flower," Blue, the spitting image of her father with her chestnut-colored hair and lone dimple that dipped into her cheek whenever she smiled, announced with a measure of pride.

"Her very favorite flower," Autumn added with a pained smile.

Hannah understood what Autumn was feeling. They had both lost sisters that they loved dearly. They were each now responsible for the raising of their niece and nephew. At least Autumn had a husband to turn to for support.

"Let's not keep you standing out here on the porch," Emma Wade said, her short, auburn curls dancing atop her shoulders as she leaned forward to open the screen door. "Come on inside."

They all moved into the house with Blue in the lead.

Hannah glanced around, finding Garrett's

parents' place to be warm and welcoming. From the pictures displayed on the walls to the crocheted throws draped over the sofa and recliner. The staircase wall had been stenciled in large black script that read Family, Faith & Love. Exactly what she would have expected from the people who had raised a man as kind and caring as Garrett.

"I wasn't sure if you would have anything to wear other than the clothes you had on when Garrett found you," Autumn said, "so I brought a few of my things for you to make use of while you are here, or until you have a chance to pick something up that suits your taste better."

Hannah was beyond touched by the gesture. "That was so kind of you, Autumn. I only had one change of clothes with me when I drove to Idaho, because I was only planning on being away for a night. So, thank you for thinking of me."

"How could I not?" she said with a warm smile. "I helped deliver your son. I can't help but feel as though we will always have a special bond."

It was true. While her own sister hadn't been able to be with her for Austin's arrival into the world, she had been blessed to have two wonderful women at her side. "I agree. I am so thankful that you and Mrs. Wade were able to be there."

"You and me both," Garrett chimed in with a grin as he removed his cowboy hat. "Barn deliveries are more my specialty."

Everyone laughed, Hannah included. Some of her sadness and fear from that morning eased with their lightheartedness.

"Let's get you settled," Emma said with a smile. "The clothes Autumn brought for you are in a bag on the bed. Come on, I'll show you to where you'll be sleeping during your stay here. It's Garrett's old room."

"I wanna show her!" Blue exclaimed as she raced to the staircase and bounced excitedly up the steps.

"Walk," Autumn called after Blue.

Garrett turned to Hannah. "I'll run your bag up, and then I'll head out to the barn while you ladies proceed with your tour."

"Your brothers have everything under control," his mother assured him. "Stay and help Hannah up the stairs, just in case she's a bit unsteady. Once we've shown her around up there, we'll go down to the kitchen and have a piece of peach pie." She smiled knowingly at her son. "I just pulled it out of the oven before you got here."

"I had intended to give Hannah a chance to settle in and get to know you and Autumn a little better without me around," he admitted. "But how could any man turn down peach pie fresh out of the oven?"

"Your brother wouldn't," Autumn said with a smile. "That's for sure."

"You don't have to worry yourself over me," Hannah protested, not wanting Garrett to change his plans again because of her. But inside she was thankful to have him there. She liked spending time with Garrett. Liked the low, soothing tone of his voice. The kindness in his smile.

He shook his head. "Can't be helped. And Mom's right. You've just had a baby. Best to take things slow. That being said, why don't we see how you handle the stairs before you try and tackle them on your own?"

She relented with a sigh, admitting, if only to herself, that she did seem to tire more easily since having her son. She supposed her body did require a little more time to recover from all the changes that it had gone through.

Placing a supportive hand at Hannah's back, Garrett escorted her up the steps behind his mother.

Autumn took up the rear.

Hannah looked up at Garrett with a grateful smile and nearly missed a step in her distraction.

"I've got you," he said, wrapping a supporting arm around her back.

She found herself leaning into his strength

when what she should be doing was insisting she do this on her own. Because that's how things were going to be once she and Austin went back to Colorado. Her father had already raised his family, and he wouldn't ask him to help her raise another. Not that he wouldn't do plenty of doting on his grandson; of that, she was certain, just as Garrett was determined to dote on her. Truth be told, it was nice having someone look after her the way he had been since coming to her rescue.

"This is the bathroom," Garrett's mother said, pausing to point it out to Hannah. "The linen closet with fresh towels and washrags is right there." She motioned toward a tall, narrow, oak cabinet door next to the bathroom's entrance.

Hannah nodded and then followed them into what Emma announced was to be her guest room during her stay there. Three walls were beige with the remaining one behind the bed done in a navy and beige plaid wallpaper. The bag Autumn had left for her sat atop the bedspread, which matched the wallpaper almost exactly. The only difference was that the quilt was edged in beige with embroidered miniature cowboy boots with spurs, and a lone boot inside a circle of beige embellished each of the two pillow shams. The bedside lamp was an antiqued bronze statue of a cowboy atop a bucking horse. A smile moved across Hannah's face as she turned to face Garrett.

"Your room is so cute."

"Let it be known that my room was not *cute* when I lived here," he said defensively. "This was all done *after* I moved out."

"I confess," his mother said. "I redid all of the boys' rooms after they moved out with things that reminded me of my sons."

"You should have seen Tucker's reaction when he saw his momma's most recent makeover to his old room," Autumn said, laughing softly.

"It's a princess room!" Blue declared, her face beaming with delight.

His mother nodded. "We added a frilly pink bedspread to Tucker's old bed, and then hung shimmery pink netting over it. But there are still reminders of Tucker in there. A wall displaying some of his rodeo pictures and ribbons, and a few framed newspaper clippings."

"Which go perfectly with the miniature crystal chandelier you switched the overhead light out for," Autumn teased with a smile.

The corner of Garrett's mouth hitched upward. "I forgot about all of that. I guess little boots aren't so bad after all."

Hannah laughed. And then she thanked the Lord for bringing the Wades into her life. Their kindness, and their humor, would undoubtedly see her through the emotional days ahead. But she was most thankful for Garrett and the happiness he stirred in her heart—one that had suffered so much hurt in recent years—whenever she was with him.

The next morning, Hannah walked into the kitchen. Emma glanced back from where she stood at the sink, washing dishes. "Good morning, dear."

"Good morning, Mrs. Wade," Hannah replied as she stepped into the room, and then catching sight of Garrett's father seated at the breakfast table, added, "Morning."

"Hannah," he greeted with a warm smile, and then stood, placing his cowboy hat atop his graying head. He walked over to plant a quick kiss on Emma's cheek. "I'll be out in the barn. Give a holler when you're ready to leave for church." With a tip of his hat to Hannah, he strode from the room.

"Emma," Garrett's mother said, drawing Hannah's attention back in her direction. "No more 'Mrs. Wade.' I've already told you there's no need for formalities here. How did you sleep last night?"

Hannah had mentioned at dinner the night before that she hoped she would be able to sleep that night, because her troubled thoughts had kept her tossing and turning until the wee hours of the morning the night before. Garrett's mother had then fixed her a cup of chamomile tea right before she turned in for the night, and it seemed to have helped. "I slept much better. Thank you again for the tea."

"You're quite welcome. I'm glad it helped." She motioned toward the kitchen table. "Have a seat. The tea water is still warm. I'll fix you a cup. Unless you'd prefer coffee instead."

"Tea is fine." She'd never acquired a liking for coffee, which she had tried a few times during her college years.

"Sugar or honey?"

"Honey."

With a nod, Garrett's mother set to making her a cup of tea. "How are you doing?"

"I'm getting my strength back," Hannah told her.

Emma looked to Hannah, a soft smile on her face. "I meant emotionally. I know you try and put up a strong front around us, but I also know how hard it is for a mother to be separated from her child."

Hannah recalled the conversation she'd had with Garrett on their way to the ranch. "I'm sure you were worried sick when Jackson was injured so badly."

"I was," she agreed. "But I was referring to a

more permanent separation. My boys had a little sister," she explained. "Her name was Mari and she was the light of our lives. But the good Lord called her home when she was only six years old. Meningitis," she said, a slight catch in her voice.

"I'm so sorry," Hannah said, her eyes filling with tears. Life was so unpredictable. Even those far too young to die did, leaving behind so much pain and sorrow. How had Emma gotten through the loss of a child, of all things? Austin had only been in her life for a few short days and Hannah knew she would be lost without him.

Garrett's mother set the cup of tea she had prepared for Hannah onto the table in front of her and then placed a comforting hand over hers. "Oh, sweetie. I didn't tell you this to make you sad. I told you because I wanted you to know that I understand how you feel, and that I am here for you if you ever need to talk."

She was so much like her own mother, Hannah thought longingly. So open and caring. Oh, how she missed her mother. "Thank you for sharing what has to be such a heartbreaking part of your life with me. I don't know what I would do if…" She let the words trail off, too afraid to speak them.

"Austin is going to grow into a big, strong young man. Just like my sons," she told her. "Have faith, sweetie."

"I'm trying," she replied with a tired sigh.

"I know you're still recovering from having given birth to that precious little boy of yours, but, if you feel up to it, Grady and I would love to have you join us for Sunday services this morning."

Church. How had she forgotten that it was Sunday?

"We'll be leaving for church at nine o'clock," Emma continued, "so you have a little over an hour to get ready if you decide to go. The boys and Autumn and Blue will all be there."

Hannah knew that despite the painful losses she had suffered in the past couple of years, she had a lot to give thanks for, and even more to pray for. She didn't understand the Lord's reasons for taking her mother the way He had, and then, so soon after, her sister and Brian. Those losses had shaken her faith, had pushed her into a place of despair and sometimes resentment toward Him. But she had found herself turning to Him during the storm, and God had listened to her prayers, sending Garrett to her rescue. And He had allowed Austin to be safely delivered, even if he wasn't physically ready to face that world yet. And He had brought Garrett into her life and allowed him to remain. If only for a very short while. It was time to make her peace with the Lord and ask for His continuing grace where her newborn son was concerned.

"As soon as I finish my tea, I'll go upstairs and get ready. Thank you for inviting me."

Emma smiled. "Tea alone is not going to help you keep your strength up. You need to eat. I made blueberry waffles for breakfast. It will only take me a second to warm some up for you if you'd like."

Hannah felt an instantaneous pull of grief and looked away, trying to quell the emotion.

"If you don't care for blueberries…" Garrett's mother began, misreading Hannah's response.

"It's not that," she replied, shaking her head. "I love blueberries. My mother used to make Heather and me blueberry pancakes every Sunday morning before we left for church when we were growing up."

The older woman's face filled with worry. "Oh, honey, I'm so sorry. I never meant to stir up sad memories for you. Let's forget the blueberries, even the waffles. I could fry you up a couple of eggs instead. They're fresh from the henhouse."

Hannah shook her head. "There's no need. Waffles will be fine." Emma looked as if she wasn't sure, so Hannah added, "I promise. If I were to avoid all the things that brought back memories of my mom and my sister, I would find myself living in a colorless world." She smiled up at Garrett's mother. "And I would be very, very hungry."

"Your words couldn't be more true," Garrett's mother said, a touch of melancholy filling her eyes. "Especially, the part about living in a colorless world. I've found that memories, both good and bad, tend to be tightly knitted together. If one attempts to tug an unwanted strand free, they risk causing some of the good strands to fall away as well. Therefore, we must learn to live with all the memories of the moments our lives have been made of and trust in God to give us the strength to continue on."

Emma understood the pain of loss. She had lost a daughter. Eyes stinging, Hannah nodded, unable to speak as she fought to hold back the tears that filled her eyes.

"Oh, honey," Emma said, moving to wrap her arms around Hannah in a warm, motherly hug. "Don't cry. You'll get me going, too."

"I'm sorry," Hannah said with a muffled sob. "I'm just feeling a little melancholy this morning."

"What can I do to help lighten your heart?" she asked as she stepped away.

Hannah brushed a single tear from her cheek. "Just having someone to really talk to helps more than you could ever know. I tend to avoid sharing my feelings with my father because he's already struggling to deal with his own emotions. But I miss him. And I really, really miss Mom and Heather."

"Of course, you do," Emma said with an empathetic smile. "There's no need for you to ever apologize for what you're feeling." She hesitated for a moment, before adding, "Hannah, I know that no one can ever replace your mother, but I would like to be there for you while you're here. Any questions you might have about being a new mother, or if you just need to talk, know that you can always come to me."

Her words touched Hannah's heart. "Thank you, Emma," she said with a soft sniffle. "Thank you for everything."

"No," she said. "Thank you. From the bottom of my heart. If you hadn't come into our lives the way you did, I don't know if Garrett would have ever forced himself to face his past and step into that hospital that day. But he did, and that's a step toward healing. I pray that my son will finally begin to move on with his life."

"Mom?" a male voice, one deliberately hushed, called out.

"In here," she called back with a smile.

A second later, Garrett stepped into the kitchen, his attention fixed on his mother who was standing directly across from him. "I know

I said I'd meet you at church, but..." His gaze slid in Hannah's direction and a smile formed across his tanned face. "You're awake?"

"I am," she said, pushing her own troubles aside as she returned his smile. *I pray that my son will finally begin to move on with his life.* What had happened in Garrett's life that he needed healing from? Not that his past was any of her business, but she knew what it felt like to bottle up the pain. She hated to think that Garrett's big, beautiful grin masked some sort of long-withheld emotional suffering.

"I'm warming her up a couple of my home-made blueberry waffles, and then Hannah and I are going to go get ready for church. Have you eaten?" she asked him.

"I've had two cups of coffee," he answered.

"So now I have to worry about both you *and* Hannah keeping your strength up?" she said, shaking her head. "Grab some silverware and a couple of napkins for you and Hannah while I fix you both a plate."

He did as she asked and then slid the items, including a bottle of spring water, in front of Hannah as he took the empty seat beside her. "I know you have tea, but I thought you might like some water as well."

She smiled up at him. "Thank you." Her thoughts grabbed on to what his mother had said about having to worry about him keeping his strength up. Did that mean there was no one special in his life to watch over him? How that was even remotely possible was beyond her. Garrett was caring and kind. And so very handsome, she thought, feeling warmth blossom in her cheeks.

His mother turned from the stove where she had warmed several waffles in the microwave just above it, and carried two plates of blueberry waffles over to the table and set them down in front of them. "Toppings are right there." She pointed to the ceramic butter dish and bottle of maple syrup that sat against the wall at the edge of the table.

"They smell delicious," Hannah said as the aroma of warm blueberries drifted upward.

"Believe me," Garrett said, cutting into one of his waffles, "they are."

Emma smiled at his response and then looked to Hannah. "I'm going to go start getting ready for church. I'm so glad you've decided to join us for this morning's services. Now, if there's anything else you need, I'm quite sure Garrett knows where to find it."

When his mother had gone, Garrett turned to Hannah. "So, you're joining us for church this morning."

"Your mother asked, and I told her I would go," she answered with a nod.

Garrett's gaze shifted to the plate in front of him as he sank the side of his fork into a syrup-covered chunk of waffle. "Are you sure you're up for it?"

Hannah said, "If you'd rather I not go, I could stay here and take a leisurely walk. I've been wanting to see more of the ranch anyhow." The last thing she wanted to do was be the cause of his having to revisit something that had caused him emotional pain in his past.

He paused between chews to look at her. Then he swallowed the bite he had taken before saying, "Why would you think I wouldn't want you to go?"

She couldn't really explain her reason, so she settled for another truth. "You've been forced to spend hours on end with me since coming to my rescue. It only stands to reason that you might prefer to spend some time alone with your family for a change."

He lowered his fork as he looked her way. "Hannah, no one is forcing me to do anything. I spend hours with you because..." He paused, as if trying to figure out the reason for himself.

"Because you're a good Christian," she finished for him, something she found both admirable and attractive. "And it's the Christian thing to do."

"Well, I like to think I'm a good Christian,

and that I'd help anyone in need. But that's not the only reason." He let his gaze drop back down to his plate. "I'm doing it because I enjoy spending time with you."

She laughed softly, but inside butterflies were fluttering about in her stomach. She felt the same way about him. "You enjoy having your work schedule all thrown off, spending long hours at the hospital and my using your shoulder to shed my tears on?" Because she had done that more than once while they were there together at the hospital.

"The answer to your question is yes," he told her as he pushed away from the table and stood. He walked over to the refrigerator and grabbed a water bottle from the top shelf.

"Why would anyone—"

"Because it feels good to be needed again," he said, closing the refrigerator door. He stood with his back to her, as if he regretted his words.

Hannah's expression softened. "It feels good to need someone," she admitted. So good. "And to know that I can trust that person to actually be there for me. I haven't trusted another man since my husband walked away from our marriage."

He turned, surprise widening his dark green eyes.

"I was married once," she admitted. "We met at the rehab facility where I worked as a physical therapist. He was an administrator in another part of the building. We dated for nearly a year before getting engaged and married six months after that. I thought we both wanted the same things in life. Especially, a family of our own, when we took our vows before God, but my husband decided not long into our marriage that he wasn't daddy material. Or husband material, as it turned out." She paused to collect herself, because revisiting the past was hard. Not because she still had feelings for her ex; she didn't. It was painful because she had wasted so much precious time trying to build a life with a man who hadn't wanted the same things and hadn't been honest enough with her or himself to realize that before they'd wed.

"Had you tried counseling?" he asked and then shook his head. "Never mind. That's not any of my business."

She didn't mind answering his question. Garrett had been so open with her. "My husband refused to waste his time going to counseling when the lines had already been drawn. I wanted children. He wanted none. To drive that fact home, he took steps medically to make sure that it could never happen, informing me of it after the fact. Then he filed for divorce, citing irreconcilable differences."

"I'm sorry you had to go through that," Garrett said solemnly. "He should have been honest with you about his feelings before marrying you."

She nodded in agreement. "At least I didn't have to go through the divorce alone. I had my parents and Heather and Brian to lean on. After my marriage ended, I moved back home with Mom and Dad, planning to stay there only a few months while I got back on my feet again. But then Mom died unexpectedly of an undiagnosed heart condition and I couldn't bring myself to leave Dad to deal with his grief all alone."

"I'm glad you and your father had each other to lean on through tough times." He searched her face, his expression one of concern. "Do you still have to see your ex at work?"

"No. He took a job elsewhere. And I took a leave after Heather and Brian died, needing time to recoup from yet another loss. Now I'm not sure I want to go back. I failed at marriage. I don't want to fail at being a parent, too."

"From what you tell me, you're not to blame for what happened," Garrett said in all seriousness. "And while I'm not a big fan of divorce, there are times when a future together is just not meant to be. Like Tucker's marriage to Summer. He never intended to marry again, hadn't even sought to put a legal end to his non-existent marriage, but life has a way of making those decisions for you when you least expect it."

"I'm glad he was able to find true happiness," Hannah said. She'd seen Tucker and Autumn together and they were very clearly two people deeply in love with each other. Something she prayed she would find for herself someday. A true and genuine, lasting kind of love. Like her parents had found together. Like Garrett's parents shared.

"You will, too, someday," he said, as if reading her thoughts.

It took her a moment to reply, to separate her thoughts from what he'd actually been responding to. "Garrett," she said with a sigh and a slight shake of her head, "how many men do you think there are out there who are actually willing to date a divorcée who has a newborn to raise?"

"They are out there, Hannah," he said. "I promise. Truth is any man would be blessed to have such a special woman come into his life. And Austin is just an added blessing. Don't ever settle for less than you deserve."

"And that would be?" she heard herself asking.

"A man who will make it his life's goal to keep a smile on your face. One who wants children, just like you. A man willing to love a child that isn't his every bit as deeply as he loves those the Lord sees fit to bless the two of you with. And he definitely has to be a man who likes dogs," he added with a lone-dimpled grin. "Because you come with those, too. Buddy and Bandit if I remember correctly."

She laughed softly. "Yes. My boys." Not only did Garrett have an impressive memory, he always seemed to have a way of lightening her mood when she truly needed it.

"And now you have one more to add to the mix," he said with a smile as he pushed away from the table. "You'd best eat up. I'll be in the doghouse with Mom if I kept you talking so long you didn't have time to get ready for church."

Hannah stabbed at another bite of waffle, while Garrett carried his fork and plate over to the sink. She expected him to set it there and then head out to the barn, but he surprised her by washing his dirty dishes. Something her husband had never done. It might have been nice to have Dave lend her a hand in the kitchen once in a while.

Garrett turned from the sink, drying his hands on a paper towel. "I'm going to head out to the barn before we leave. If you want, you can ride with me. We can go straight from church for the hospital."

She wanted to jump at his offer, never passing up an opportunity to see her son. But Emma had extended the invitation. "I wouldn't feel right riding to church with you after accepting your mother's invitation to go with them."

He smiled. "Believe me, it's not the method of getting you to church that will make Mom's day, but the fact that you will be joining us for this morning's services. She'll want to introduce you to everyone."

"All the same, I would feel better about it if I were to ask her first."

"If it will set your mind at ease," he said, "run it past my mother. You can let me know when it's time to leave. Now eat."

"Eating," Hannah told him with a laugh as she placed another syrup-covered bite into her mouth. She watched him go, a smile on her face. It was nice, in a way, to have someone looking out for her. In her case, several someones, as the Wades were a very caring family. Her father would like them very much. Lord knows, Garrett had already scored major points with him by saving her life and the baby's.

As she sat alone, finishing her breakfast, Hannah thought about everything that had happened since the flood. She'd given birth to a beautiful baby boy who already owned her heart, and then spent two nights tossing and turning in her hospital bed because Austin was so small and frail, and fighting to breathe. And then she'd learned that he needed even more specialized care because of the jaundice that had set in. In those three days, Garrett had so selflessly taken time away from his own life to run her back and forth to the hospital to look in on her and Austin. Who would have thought it could get any harder? But it had, the moment she'd left the hospital without the baby she'd carried with her for so long. Not even two whole days and it felt like she'd been away from Austin a lifetime.

How many more days would she be without the precious child she'd brought into this world? How many more days would she be dependent on Garrett and his family? Not that they'd ever, not even for one second, made her feel like she was an imposition. If anything, she'd found herself enveloped in the caring warmth of Garrett's family. They treated her as if she were one of their own, which touched her deeply.

And Blue, with her adorable curiosity and sweet nature, had stolen Hannah's heart from that very first moment. Her unexpected questions and adorable comments had not only put a smile on her face, it had helped put Hannah at ease as she was welcomed into Emma and Grady Wade's home.

For all the bad that had come her way the past couple of years, Hannah still couldn't help but feel blessed. Blessed to have had the Wades come into her life. Blessed to have made a special connection with Emma and Autumn that she hoped would carry on once she'd returned to Steamboat Springs. And blessed to have Garrett as her anchor during the stormy weather that was her life.

Chapter Six

Hannah stood beside Garrett on the front sidewalk just outside of the church, smiling politely as Emma Wade introduced her to several of her close friends following that morning's service. Everyone had been so warm and welcoming to her, with several of the women offering advice on caring for a newborn that Hannah appreciated more than they would ever know. Once she went back to Steamboat Springs, she was going to be on her own with the raising of her son.

A man in a lawman's uniform came over to them. "Tucker," he greeted with a nod before turning to Hannah. "You must be Miss Sanders," he said, removing his cowboy hat.

She nodded and then looked to Garrett.

"Hannah, this is Sheriff Dawson."

"Justin," he corrected. "Since I'm not here on official business. I was just passing by on my way back from a one-car accident I got called out to on the outskirts of town. Figured I would stop and say a quick hello."

"Speaking of getting called out," Garrett said, pulling his phone out of the front pocket of his dress pants. "I forgot to turn my ringer back on after church." As he did so, he glanced at the screen with a frown.

"Something wrong?" Hannah asked.

"Probably not," he said, his attention fixed on the phone. "But it appears that I missed a call while we were attending this morning's service."

"If you need to return the call, I don't mind waiting," Hannah assured him with a smile. "Truth is, I'd feel better if I knew that I wasn't keeping you from your work completely."

He looked to Hannah apologetically. "I won't be long."

"Take however long you need," she told him, meaning it. He had done so much for her, setting a large part of his own life aside. He'd been more attentive to her feelings and her needs than her husband had ever been. Why couldn't she have met Garrett first, when her life was simpler? Happier. Hannah quickly pushed thoughts of Garrett aside. She was going through an emotional time and he was being kind to her like the good Christian man he was. Nothing more.

"No need to worry, Garrett," the sheriff said.

"I'll keep her entertained until you get back. I've got all kinds of stories to tell her about you and your brothers while we wait."

She didn't miss the playful grin Garrett's friend aimed in his direction. "This sounds like it could get interesting," Hannah said, unable to resist joining in on the fun.

Garrett shot a warning glance in his friend's direction and then his gaze shifted back to Hannah. "I really do need to see what this call was about. Don't believe a word he has to say about me. None of it's true."

She laughed. "I'll be sure to keep that in mind."

"I won't be long," he told her. Then, bringing the phone to his ear, he stepped into the parking lot, away from the chattering church crowd.

"So, if we go by your not believing a word I have to say, I should begin with telling you what a nice guy Garrett Wade is."

Hannah couldn't help herself, she laughed, drawing a few glances their way, Garrett's included as he paced an empty section of the parking lot.

"In all seriousness, though," Justin said, "Garrett Wade is one of the best men I know, but I suppose I don't have to convince you of that. Not after he put his own life in harm's way to save yours."

"And my son's," she said, finally getting a little more comfortable with referring to Heather's little boy as her own. "And you're right. I need no convincing where Garrett is concerned. He's gone above and beyond what most people would have done to help me out. I'm truly blessed to have had him come into my life. Even if it's only for a short while."

"Speaking of your son," the sheriff said, "how is he doing? Garrett told me they were going to keep him in their care until he's a little stronger."

She forced a cheery smile. "He's holding his own and getting stronger every day." Her smile was merely a front for the fear she felt when she allowed all the what-ifs to creep into her thoughts. And, despite all the extra prayers she had sent heavenward while sitting in church that morning, Hannah knew she wouldn't feel completely at ease until she had Austin home with her for good. Visits to the hospital, which she made every day, thanks to Garrett, weren't the same as having her baby home where she could watch him sleep, could hold him anytime she felt the need. It was a constant reminder that he wasn't strong enough, healthy enough, to be in her life the way she longed for him to be.

"I'm glad to hear it," he said and then reached into the front pocket of his uniform shirt and withdrew a card. "As soon as you're feeling up to it, I'd like to get together with you to finish the report I started on your accident. For my records and for insurance purposes. There are parts of it that you have to supply answers for."

A frown overtook her smile. "I'm sorry to have held your paperwork up. I never even gave that any thought."

"It's not like your mind hasn't been focused elsewhere."

She nodded. "True. But you have a job to do."

"Another day or two won't make a bit of difference." He handed her the card he'd pulled out of his pocket. "My number is on there. Just give me a call when it's convenient, and I'll run out to the ranch to get your information."

"I'll call you tomorrow to set up a time. I'm already keeping Garrett from his normal work schedule. I won't be responsible for keeping you from doing your job, too."

"Garrett is self-employed," he told her. "He's free to adjust his vet and ranching schedules as need be."

She was grateful that he was a close friend of the Wades, and that it was a small town, otherwise she might have been answering his questions from her hospital bed. Lord knew she'd had enough on her mind in the hospital without having had to relive her near-death experience on top of it.

"Sounds good."

"Justin," Garrett's sister-in-law greeted in that sweet Southern twang of hers as she came over to join them. "We missed you at church this morning." Having witnessed the ease with which Autumn interacted with others at Sunday services that morning, Hannah found it hard to remember that she had only been a part of the Bent Creek community for a short while.

"I took the morning shift, so Wyatt and Lloyd could join their families at church."

"From what I've heard, and from more than one Wade brother mind you, all you do is work," Autumn said with a disapproving frown. "How are you ever gonna have a family of your own to attend church with if you're working all the time?"

He chuckled. "Maybe you ought to be giving this scolding to Jackson. As far as I know he's not married yet either. Besides, someone's got to protect this town. In fact, I was on my way back to the office after getting called out to a single-car accident when I saw that church had let out. I figured I would stop and say a quick hello."

"No one was injured, I pray," Hannah said.

"No," he said with a shake of his head. "The car sustained a small dent in its fender, and the runaway cow it crossed paths with sustained an even bigger dent to its pride."

"It's so nice to live in a place where the only real crime is an occasional yard-break by a cantankerous animal," Autumn said with a smile.

Justin chuckled, nodding in agreement. "Our town is definitely blessed with truly good people." He glanced toward Garrett who was pacing the other end of the parking lot, and then turned back to Hannah. "Garrett looks to be pretty wrapped up in something. I need to get going. Can you tell him I'll catch up with him this week sometime?"

"I'll tell him," she said with a smile. "It was nice to meet you."

"The pleasure was all mine," he replied, and then, with a tip of his cowboy hat, he walked away.

"He's so nice, but like Garrett," Autumn began as they watched the sheriff walk away, "he can't get past the heartache to find love again."

Hannah looked to Autumn. "Garrett had his heart broken?" Even as she asked the question, she had to wonder how any woman could walk away from a man as good and giving as Garrett was. Poor Garrett. Her heart went out to him, knowing all too well how it felt to have one's heart trampled over. No wonder he'd been so sympathetic to her own failed relationship.

"He doesn't talk about it," his sister-in-law explained, "but Garrett was head over heels for a girl he dated when he was in high school. Chances are they would have gone on to get married, but she got sick and was diagnosed with leukemia. He spent hours on end with her at the hospital as she went through aggressive treatments, but it wasn't enough. I think Garrett's dreams died right along with Grace."

Hannah gasped, her eyes welling with tears. "How awful for Garrett and that girl's family."

"Please don't say anything to him about her," Autumn pleaded. "It's not something he talks about. I only know because Tucker and his momma told me what happened when I was teasing Garrett about needing to find him and Jackson women to make their lives complete. Garrett walked away without a word, later apologizing for it, but I knew then why he had reacted the way he had."

Her heart ached for Garrett and the emotional pain he had suffered, to have loved and lost so young. And he must have cared very deeply for Grace to have shut his heart off the way he had in the years since. Would he ever get to a place where he could move on and open his heart up to love again? Garrett deserved to find happiness after what he'd gone through with Grace. Something came to her at that moment. "Autumn, was Grace at the same hospital Austin is at?"

"Yes."

She had no idea how Garrett had been able to deal with being there again. Especially for hours on end, which he had done while Hannah had been in the hospital.

"Which is why we were surprised when he insisted on being the one to take you to the hospital that day," Autumn remarked. "If he hadn't been able to bring himself to step through those doors to check in on his brother during Jackson's stay there, what if he couldn't do it for you once he got you to the hospital? That's why Tucker and Jackson followed the two of you there as soon as they'd put the fence back together."

"They were at the hospital, too? I had no idea."

"Neither did Garrett," she replied. "They waited outside long enough to know you'd have somebody there for you, just in case Garrett needed them to take over."

But Garrett had seen things through, despite the pain it must have caused him to do so. The more she learned about Garrett, the more deeply he weaved his way into her heart. "I had no idea. That was so thoughtful of them. But I feel awful that Garrett had to do something so painful to him because of me."

"Don't feel bad," Autumn told her. "He chose to be there for you. And we are all thanking the good Lord for bringing you into our lives, most especially into Garrett's, because your being here has forced him to push past some of that pain he's held in for so long. In fact, I think as hard as it has been, it's been healing for him."

Hannah had no chance to reply as Garrett returned to where he'd left them standing on the sidewalk. She looked up into his handsome face, noting the lines of worry knitting his brows. It was clear that the lengthy call had been anything but an uplifting one. "Everything okay?" she asked.

"I'm afraid not," he said with a troubled sigh.

"What happened?" Autumn asked, her expression every bit as serious as Garrett's.

"One of Brad Wilson's cows got out of its pasture, a young calf, actually, and got struck by a car."

Hannah looked to Autumn. "That must be the single-car accident Justin told us about."

"The good news is that the injury appears to be below the calf's knee, so there's a good chance she won't have to be put down. Bad news is I'm not going to be able to run you to the hospital like we'd planned. I have to head out to the Wilson farm and tend to the calf's leg. You can ride home with Mom and Dad, and I will run you to the hospital later."

"Of course, you need to go see to that poor cow," Hannah said without hesitation. "I know

Austin is in good hands. Jessica will be there with him this morning and part of the afternoon."

"Jessica?" Autumn said, looking to Hannah.

"One of the nurses in the neonatal care unit Hannah's gotten to know pretty well," Garrett explained.

"There's no need for Hannah to go back to the ranch," Autumn said. "Tucker has to see to a few things at the main barn after we get home. Hannah can ride with us to our place, and then she and I can go to the hospital together in my car."

Hannah was about to tell her that she could wait until later when Garrett got home, but then she recalled the conversation she'd had with Autumn while he was on the phone. If she could get to the hospital without his having to take her, then she would. "If you're sure."

Autumn waved a hand, shooing that thought away. "Nonsense. I'm gonna be sitting at home twiddling my thumbs while Tucker is down at the barn. I'd much rather be spending the afternoon with you and seeing that sweet little boy of yours."

"Thanks, Autumn," Garrett said with a grateful smile. He looked to Hannah. "I'll see you later."

She watched as he walked away in long, hurried strides.

"I'll go get Tucker," Autumn said, starting back toward the church.

Emma came over to join Hannah. "Garrett's leaving without you?"

"He got called out to tend to an injured cow. Autumn's going to take me to see Austin today."

"I see. You know I'd really like to see that little one of yours again," Emma said. "If I took you a day or two a week it would give Garrett a chance to work on ranching business, and me a chance to spend some time with that sweet baby of yours."

"I'd like that," Hannah replied, realizing at that moment that Austin would grow up without the warm love of a grandmother. One he could spend Sunday afternoons with. Bake cookies with. There would be no aunts or uncles. But he would have a grandfather who would adore him, she thought, trying to focus on what she did have.

"Then we'll arrange it," Emma said.

Hannah couldn't help but wonder if Emma was offering because she really did want to spend time with the little boy she had helped to bring into this world, or if it was more a mother's attempt to keep her son from having to do something Hannah now knew was an emotional hardship for him. Either way, it was what needed to be done, because Hannah would do anything to keep him from spending more time than necessary in a place that held such sad memories for him. Even if it meant her spending less time with Garrett, a man she'd grown surprisingly fond of in the short time she'd known him. A man she'd come to care very deeply about. And because of that, she would do whatever it took to keep him from having to face the pain of his past, something he did every time he took her to see Austin.

"I have to say that my dress looks much better on you than it ever did on me," Autumn said with a smile as they walked out to her car.

Hannah glanced down at the high-waisted, wispy skirted dress. "It definitely helps to hide my post-baby belly."

Autumn snorted. "What belly? If I hadn't been there for the delivery, I would never guess that you gave birth only days ago. I was referring to the color. Green is so much better suited to your hair color. And it matches, or at least nearly matches, your green eyes."

They settled into the front seats of Autumn's car.

"You can have that dress if you like," Autumn said as she buckled her seat belt. "I will be too big for it anyway very soon." She looked to Hannah. "Which is another reason I wanted to drive you to the hospital. To talk about having babies."

Hannah's eyes widened. "You're pregnant?"

The smile on Autumn's face doubled in size. "Yes. But no one knows yet. We wanted to wait until I get a little further along in my pregnancy before making the announcement. But I have so many questions. And who better to talk to about what to expect than you?"

"Your mother?" Hannah suggested. That's what she would have done if she'd had the opportunity to do so. And she was certainly no expert on the matter. She hadn't even gone through a complete pregnancy with Austin.

Autumn's smiled faded slightly. "She wasn't in my life much when I was growing up. Summer and I were raised by our grandma who is no longer with us."

"I'm sorry. I lost my mother a little over a year ago." Hannah was discovering so many things they had in common. But she still wished Autumn would turn to someone more knowledgeable about having babies. Someone who'd had more practice. Although it meant a lot that Autumn had felt comfortable enough to confide in her. Like a true friend. "What about Emma? She's given birth many times. I've only done it once, and even that didn't go quite as expected."

"Tucker's momma had her babies decades

ago," Autumn said matter-of-factly. "So, while she knows all about raising little ones, she's not as up on the current recommended pregnancy dos and don'ts as you are."

She supposed Autumn had a point. A lot of things had changed since Emma had given birth to her sons. "I'd be happy to answer any questions you might have," she told her. "As long as I have the answers for them." How could she refuse?

Autumn's smile returned. "I would really appreciate it. And I promise not to overwhelm you with too many questions. I know you're still recovering from having your own baby."

Hannah laughed softly. "I highly doubt a few questions are going to tax my strength."

Autumn glanced her way. "Seriously, though," she said, "if I get too carried away with baby talk, feel free to redirect our conversation elsewhere. It's just that I know I've already been talking Tucker's ears off with my endless chatter about our baby and we've only just found out we're expecting. Not that my husband isn't every bit as excited as I am. He's just a lot calmer about it. But then I guess, if you spent years riding horses and bulls bareback, having a baby must seem like a walk in the park."

"That's only because Tucker doesn't have to do any of the carrying part," Hannah pointed out.

Autumn nodded. "True. He only had to hang on for eight seconds. I'll be hanging on for another seven or so months. But I can handle that, I think, as long as he or she is healthy."

Hannah prayed Autumn's pregnancy went full term. She would never wish what she was going through with her own son on any mother. The separation. The waking every morning feeling fearful that things might have taken a turn for the worse and, if they had, that she wouldn't be there to say goodbye. Funny, but she found herself thinking at that moment that Garrett would never allow anything bad to happen. To Austin or her. That, with him by her side, she could face anything. If only she could keep him by her side forever.

"Hannah?" Autumn said worriedly.

She snapped out of her thoughts and looked to Autumn.

"I'm so sorry for being so unthinking when I spoke, with that precious little boy of yours dealing with health issues brought about by his coming too early. I never meant to be insensitive."

"Of course, you didn't," Hannah said with a reassuring smile. "It's only natural for a mother-to-be to hope her child is born free of any health complications. Heather had prayed for that same thing when we found out the invitro fertilization had worked, because all she had known with her pregnancies was loss. I prayed for the Lord to allow me to keep my sister's baby safe." She looked to Autumn. "I never thought to pray to Him to keep her and Brian safe. If only..." She sighed, feeling the tears well up in her eyes.

"It was their time to go, Hannah," Autumn said, compassion in her voice. "Just like with my sister. There were times I wondered why her and not me. Summer had a little girl to raise. I didn't have anyone. I've learned that questions don't always have answers. We just have to learn to accept God's will and live our lives as fully as He will allow us to during our time here on earth. Focus on our blessings, so to speak. And bc the best second mother to Blue as I can be."

"Second mother," Hannah repeated in thought. "I have been so torn over having Austin call me Aunt Hannah or Mommy, something he should have been calling my sister."

"But she is gone, and *you* will be raising Austin," Autumn told her. "With Blue, she had been raised by her momma for several years before losing her. I was fine with her continuing to call me Aunt Autumn. But recently she's been slipping a Momma in here and there instead. I think it makes sense to her because Tucker is her daddy and we're a family now. In your case, you are the only momma your son is ever gonna know. I think your sister would understand your becoming her son's mother. She trusted you with his life from the very beginning, and I'm sure she's watching down over the both of you, grateful that Austin has you in his life."

Tears blurred Hannah's vision as she looked at her new friend. Even if they'd only known each other for just a very short time. In a way, Autumn helped to fill a void left in her heart after Heather had died. She'd missed those sisterly talks, that special bond she'd shared with her sister so very much.

"I'm sorry," Hannah said, turning to look out the passenger side window as she brushed a lone tear from her cheek. "Crying seems to be my thing right now," she said with a forced laugh. "Just ask Garrett. I've cried on his shoulder more than I've ever cried in my life. The poor man."

"I'm sure Tucker can relate," Autumn said with a gentle smile. "My emotions are all over the place these days. But from what I've read it's normal during pregnancy and after giving birth, until a woman's body has a chance to return to its normal state."

Hannah nodded with a soft sniffle.

"And you probably still have a lot of grief you haven't dealt with," Autumn said knowingly.

"You're probably right," Hannah said. "I couldn't grieve, wouldn't grieve, around my father. I didn't want to be the cause of any more pain for him."

"Well, maybe you can do some emotional healing while you're in Bent Creek. It took my bringing Blue here to meet her daddy to force my own grief over Summer's dying to the surface. The town, the people, are all so kind and giving. And Tucker's family," she said, shaking her head, "they are the best. I came here determined to prove him an unfit daddy so I could raise Blue myself in Cheyenne, but they welcomed me with open arms. I wasn't their enemy. I was a part of their family because I was family to Blue." This time it was Autumn who was tearing up. "See what you started," she said on choked laughter.

Hannah couldn't help but smile.

"I will tell you," Autumn said, "it was a healing thing to let all that built-up pain go. For both my heart and soul. Just as it will be for you when you are ready to let it go."

"I want to get to that point," Hannah admitted. "But, right now, all I can focus on is my *son* and how unprepared I am for what comes next. I was more than ready to carry a child for my sister, having read all the books on pregnancy I could get my hands onto. But I never thought about what came after giving birth. That was for Heather and Brian to prepare for. And then they died, and I was too overcome by shock and grief to think beyond the gaping hole their deaths had left in my life to focus on what I would need once their son was born. I don't have anything but a crib, which my sister and Brian bought as soon as they found out they were expecting."

"Didn't any of your friends have a baby shower for you?"

She shook her head. "Most of my friends from high school moved away, just as I did after I got married. After moving back home following my divorce, I spent most of my time with my family. Heather was my best friend. I was supposed to have thrown her a baby shower," Hannah said, her voice catching. "Not have someone throw one for me."

Autumn reached over to give Hannah's hand a squeeze. "We'll just have to go baby shopping while you're here. Besides, showers are over-rated," she added with a flutter of her hand. "You have to play all those silly games."

"Silly games?" Hannah asked. "I've never actually been to one, so I honestly have no idea what goes on." She had just assumed that it was a cake and some pretzel and chips with dip, followed by the opening of gifts.

"Well, you aren't missing anything," Autumn said a little too nonchalantly, and Hannah knew she was just saying that for her benefit. "No, I take that back. The food is great. Some sort of sandwiches, veggie trays, fruit, chips and dip, and, of course, cake. But there are usually two or three games played during the shower. One of them involves the guests cutting off a piece of string to a length they think will fit around the expectant momma's belly. Whoever's string is closest to the real thing wins a prize of some sort."

Hannah studied Autumn's face for a moment, trying to determine if she was teasing her or not. She seemed serious enough. "They really do that?" She was suddenly grateful she hadn't had anyone to throw her a baby shower, because she had gotten quite round with Austin.

"They do," Autumn insisted. "Believe me. I've played it at several showers. Now that I'm pregnant, I'm rethinking the humor I once found in playing that particular game. I mean, come on, what woman really wants people guessing their baby-expanded waist size? Why don't people just bring pumpkins to the shower and the one that looks closest to the size of the pregnant woman's belly wins the prize?"

Hannah laughed. "Maybe because that would only go over well in the fall."

Autumn's laughter filled the car.

"Autumn," Hannah said, growing serious, "had Garrett planned to have a family with Grace?"

"I couldn't say for sure," she replied. "I only know what Tucker's told me. But if he loved Grace as deeply as I think he did, then I would think he had hoped to have a family with her someday. Why?"

She wanted so badly to confess her growing feelings for Garrett to Autumn. To ask if she felt there was any chance he might open up his heart again. Only she couldn't bring herself to do so. "Because he deserves to find happiness again. Even in the short time I've known him, I can tell he'd be a devoted and loving husband. And I've seen him with Blue. He'd make such a wonderful father."

"I couldn't agree more. If only you lived closer. I think you would be good for Garrett. And we could easily become the best of friends."

Oh, how she wished she did, too. Not only for the friendship Autumn could offer her, but for the unexpected connection she and Garrett had made. Maybe he was just being kind because that was who he was, or felt duty bound, as a faithful Christian, to keep her company during her brief stay there, but it felt like more than that to her. All she could do was enjoy every moment spent with Garrett during her stay there, knowing it would all come to an end in a few short weeks, because her life was in Steamboat Springs, watching over her father and raising her sister's son.

"Not back yet, huh?"

Garrett turned to find Tucker leaning against the open barn door. He shook his head. No sense trying to pretend he was doing anything other than watching for Hannah and Autumn's return. "I should have gone straight to the hospital after I finished up at the Wilson ranch." But his brothers had convinced him to take a step back and give Autumn and Hannah a chance to spend some time together. He might not have given in to their suggestion if their mother hadn't put in her two cents, telling him that sometimes a woman just needed another woman to talk to. Especially, after going through something as life changing as having a baby. So he'd gone home, washed up, and then had driven out to the main ranch to wait for his sister-in-law and Hannah's return with news of her son.

"You did the right thing," his brother told him.

Then why didn't the "right thing" not feel so right to him? "They've been gone a long while. What if there was a problem with her baby? An emergency," he added worriedly.

"Autumn would have called to let me know,

and she hasn't. So stop watching the second-hand sweep by on your watch and find something useful to do."

Tucker was right. Hannah was in good hands, and there was always something that could be done at the ranch. But it was hard to wrap his head around anything other than Hannah. Thoughts of her smile. Her soft laughter. Her willingness to use his shoulder to lean on, to cry on. Her son. Reining in his wandering mind, Garrett said, "I'll go check on the horses we'll be taking on the road." They had been separated out from the other horses so they could be fed a little extra, and so they would be easier to round up when the time came to load them onto one of the tractor trailers they used to transport their stock to the rodeo.

"Garrett..." his brother said, pushing away from the barn door to follow Garrett to his truck.

He glanced over at his youngest brother, his expression no longer filled with humor.

"I know I was just a kid when Grace died, but I saw how hard it was on you." Tucker hadn't even started high school at the time.

"Tucker," he said with a frown, not wanting to go there.

"Even talking about her isn't easy for you," his brother went on. "We all know that. And Jackson and I both said we would have done the same thing if we were in your shoes."

But they hadn't been. He'd been the one who had lost the only woman, girl actually, that he'd ever loved. "I didn't do anything."

"That's my point," Tucker said. "You shut down emotionally for a long time after Grace's death and I found myself missing the brother I once looked up to. You were closed off, determined to keep everyone at arm's length. At least, emotionally."

"At first, I couldn't feel," Garrett confessed with a sigh. "I was numb inside. And then when my emotions started to thaw, I felt guilt. How could I even consider moving on, when Grace should have been the one I was moving on with? It was easier to sit back and do nothing. Feel nothing."

"We figured as much. I have to admit that it's been hard watching you in your self-imposed isolation where any real relationships were concerned, knowing where it stemmed from, but wanting so much more for you. I gave thanks to God for bringing Blue into our lives for so many reasons, one of them being the change it made in you. You smile more now. Laugh more. It's like you finally gave yourself permission to live life again." His brother looked down, digging the toe of his boot in the dirt, before looking up again. "What I'm trying to say is that you deserve to be happy. Grace would have wanted you to move on, to find someone who makes you feel that happiness again."

Garrett's first thought when his brother spoke of happiness was of Hannah, and then that all-too-familiar feeling of guilt threatened to surface. "If you're thinking about setting me up with someone…"

"Not a chance," his brother replied. "I think you're perfectly capable of finding someone on your own who can make you every bit as happy as you deserve to be. In fact, maybe you already have." Turning, Tucker strode back into the barn, chuckling as he went.

Maybe you already have.

Garrett stood pondering his brother's parting words. Had he? His heart took off in a gallop at the thought and his immediate reaction was to find some way to regain control of that runaway horse.

Autumn's car came rolling up the drive at that moment, saving him from his thoughts. He cut across the yard toward the house to greet them.

Hannah waved to him with a bright smile as she stepped from the car, sending that horse careening right out of his emotional gate once again. Then she bent into the car to retrieve several shopping bags from the backseat.

Autumn closed the driver's side door and looked to Hannah. "I look forward to doing this again soon."

"Me, too," Hannah replied.

Autumn turned and set off for the barn, passing Garrett on the way. "She's all yours."

All mine. That thought set a little too comfortably with him. Garrett looked to Hannah as he moved toward her. She wasn't his. He wasn't even looking for someone to be "his." But if he were, Hannah would be the kind of woman he would look for.

Garrett reached for the packages. "Let me get those for you."

"Thank you."

He glanced down at the numerous bags and then back to Hannah as they made their way to the house. "They put a mall in the hospital I wasn't aware of?"

She laughed softly. "No. Autumn and I stopped by the mall on our way back to the ranch to pick up a few baby things."

He lifted the weighty bags. "A few?"

"I might have gotten carried away," Hannah said, flushing. "And I picked up some post-baby clothes for me."

"Your taking time to shop tells me Austin is doing well," he said knowingly. Hannah wouldn't have done so if that weren't the case.

Her bright smile widened even further. "He's doing very well," she told him. "Jessica said they expect to be able to remove the bilirubin lights within a day or two. And his lungs are strengthening."

Garrett grinned at the news. "I told you he was a fighter."

"He is," she said proudly. "And I think he's starting to know the sound of my voice."

"Of course, he does," he said. "He's listened to it for the past seven or so months."

"You know what I mean," she said, laughing once again.

The sound of her laughter wrapped around him, did something to him. *Maybe you already have.* Tucker's earlier words came rushing back to him and Garrett went into immediate denial. He couldn't have found the woman meant to make him happy, because he wasn't looking. He was only watching over Hannah and her son until her father was well enough to come to Bent Creek to take over the duty himself.

Garrett stole another glance at Hannah, whose pretty face radiated her joy at the news she'd received regarding her son's improving health. Watching over her felt like the farthest thing from a duty to him, but he had to force himself to think of it that way. Hannah and her son would be leaving, and if Austin continued to improve as steadily as he had been, as they had all prayed he would, that day would come very soon. But he was also well-aware that setbacks happened. If Austin ended up having to remain in the hospital longer than expected, it would tear Hannah up inside. Him, too. Even if bringing Austin home meant letting Hannah go.

"Would you like to take a drive?" Garrett asked as they stepped up onto his parents' front porch. He reached for the door. "I could give you a tour of the place."

"As much as I would love to, I'm going to have to ask for a rain check on your offer," Hannah replied. "It's been such a full day with church, and then the hospital, and then shopping with Autumn. I can barely keep my eyes open."

"Of course," he said, doing his best not to show his disappointment. He really had missed spending time with her that afternoon. But he understood. "Maybe one day this week we'll take that drive. Weather permitting." Storms were expected to be moving into the area over the next several days.

"I look forward to it," she said, smiling up at him.

He looked down into her thickly lashed, pale green eyes and returned her smile. "Me, too."

She looked up at him. "I missed visiting with you today."

There went that funny feeling again. Ignoring it, Garrett said, "I wish I could have been there with you."

"I know you would have been if you could have," she told him. "Speaking of which, how is Mr. Wilson's cow?"

"She'll live," he said. "Hopefully, she learned a valuable lesson today. That the grass isn't always greener on the other side. Especially, when the 'other side' consists of a well-traveled road."

Once again, her lilting laughter rose up around him. "A very good lesson to remember. I'm glad she's going to be all right. But then, with you watching over her, how could she be anything but?"

His being there hadn't helped Grace.

"Hannah," his mother said in greeting as she stepped from the kitchen.

"Hello, Emma."

"How's that darling little one of yours doing?"

"Better than expected," Hannah answered. "Thus the shopping bags Garrett offered to carry in for me. Autumn and I stopped by the mall after seeing Austin."

"Ah, good," his mother said. "Nothing more therapeutic than a girls' day out shopping."

"It was nice," Hannah agreed. "But I didn't go as much for me as I did for Austin. When I told Autumn that I didn't have any baby things bought yet, she suggested we stop and pick up a few things. Because, with God's good grace, my son will be coming home from the hospital very soon."

"Amen to that," his mother said.

"You didn't have *any* baby items bought?" Garrett said in surprise.

"Not until today," she admitted. "Now I at least have a few of the essentials I'll be needing, along with a half dozen or so sleepers. Oh, and I do have a crib. Heather and Brian bought one less than a week after they found out they were finally going to be parents. As for anything else, well, I thought I would have more time to prepare for Austin's arrival."

"Our children do like to surprise us on occasion," Emma said.

"With grandchildren, to give one example," Garrett muttered.

"One grandchild," his mother corrected. "And Blue was the best surprise I have ever received."

Me, too, Garrett thought. His niece was the light of his life. Tucker was beyond blessed to have her. He'd never allowed himself to consider what it might be like to have a child of his own to love and to raise after losing Grace, but from the moment he'd first held Austin in his arms, those thoughts had begun nudging at him. But it had been the talk he'd had with his brother that had forced him to rethink the way he'd been living his life. Maybe someday he could have the family he had once dreamed of.

Hannah turned to face him. "I'll take my packages now. Thank you for carrying them in for me," she said as he handed them over to her.

"Anytime," he said.

"I'm on my way upstairs to fold a basket of laundry I carried up to my room a short while ago," his mother told Hannah. "Let me take a couple of those bags for you."

"You don't have to do that," Hannah tried to protest, but Emma was already relieving her of two of her purchases. Then she started up the stairs with them.

"I'll leave these on your bed," she called back over her shoulder. "See you at dinner this evening, Garrett."

"I'll be there," he replied, and then found himself searching for some other small piece of conversation to throw out there to stall their having to part ways. But there wasn't really anything he could say that wouldn't sound exactly like what it was meant to be—an attempt to stall his departure. So he steeled himself, tipped his hat to her and then headed back out to the barn to find something to keep his thoughts on anything other than his parents' beautiful houseguest.

Chapter Seven

That whole week, storms rolled in and out of Bent Creek, postponing their tour of the ranch. Garrett looked to the window, thanking heaven above that the rain had finally passed. Nothing but clear skies stretched over the distant mountains. That meant he would finally be able to give Hannah the tour of the ranch he had promised her. He'd found himself eagerly looking forward to sharing that part of his life with her. Something beyond the limited view of the ranch that she'd seen from the road as they traveled back and forth to the hospital to see her son.

Her son. His namesake. The child Garrett had found himself bonding with more and more with each passing day when he accompanied Hannah to the hospital to see him. He turned from the window and looked to the specialized crib Austin had spent most of his time in since coming into the world. Then his gaze came to rest on Hannah, who sat next to it in one of the neonatal unit's rocking chairs. She was holding her son, her love-filled gaze fixed on the tiny infant she cradled in her arms.

If one's heart could melt, Garrett was certain his would have. It was a memory he knew would remain in his thoughts long after they went back to the life that awaited them in Steamboat Springs. He had started off bringing her to the hospital because she had no one else to take her there. Because he felt a certain responsibility to do so. But as the days went on, he found himself looking forward to their time, watching Hannah with her son, whom she was now able to hold for short periods, and of getting to hold Austin himself.

While holding her son made him long for something he would never have, it was also a reminder of how precious life really was. That he needed to appreciate the time the good Lord chose to grant him and live it to its fullest. Something he hadn't done after losing Grace. But that had changed with Hannah's unexpected arrival in his life. It had happened slowly. Emotional baby steps so to speak. But he was ready to admit he no longer wanted to be alone. He wanted what Tucker had, a family to love and to love him.

Hannah looked up and graced him with one of her pretty smiles, which she did on occasion, perhaps wanting him to know she hadn't forgotten he was there. Or maybe she just wanted to pass on the joy she felt as she held her son. Either way, her smile was always a welcome thing. He'd been there for Hannah those times she had, fearing for her too-small son, given in to the tears. He'd been there when she'd struggled to keep her eyes open, exhausted by everything she'd been through. And he'd been there when she'd needed to talk. Sometimes about her past. Sometimes about simple things.

There were so many things about Grace he no longer remembered, or maybe he'd blocked them from his mind because it had always hurt his heart to think about her. He'd done more thinking and talking about Grace since Hannah had come into his life than he had for the past seventeen years. Doing so had been surprisingly cathartic.

It was Hannah who had been first and foremost on his mind since coming into his life. He knew her favorite color was red. The one place she longed to travel to was anywhere she'd be able to see the Northern Lights, where their brilliant colors reached far up into the heavens. And her favorite movie was *P.S. I Love You*, because it was about two people who loved each other beyond measure, and the willingness to let love in again after one's first true love was lost.

At least, that's what he'd garnered from the online search he'd done afterward to see what the movie was about. When Hannah had absently mentioned it, she'd quickly changed the subject, but he'd found himself wanting to know more about this movie that had resonated so deeply. Then he knew why she'd tried to redirect the conversation. It had been to protect his feelings. That kind gesture meant more than she could ever know, but like the main character in that movie he knew it was time to move on.

"Would you like to hold him?" she asked with a warm smile. "You haven't held him since that stormy afternoon at Jackson's."

That's because it had felt too right, holding Austin in his arms that day. Like he was meant to be there. "If you don't mind giving him up for a bit," he replied with a widening grin as he eyed the infant asleep in her arms. That day he'd run from the rightness of it. Today he was ready to open himself up to new feelings. To possibilities.

"I don't mind sharing him with you," Hannah replied, tenderness in her eyes as she handed her son over to him. They'd already washed their hands when they'd first stepped into the neonatal care room. She pushed up from the rocking chair and stepped aside so Garrett could settle himself into it.

"He's growing more and more every day," Garrett said as he began to rock in a slow, easy movement. "In fact, I think that's a whisker I see sprouting from his chin," he teased, making light when the moment felt anything but. Emotion had knotted thick in his throat.

Hannah laughed softly as she leaned over them, admiring her son. "Won't be long before he's asking for a cowboy hat and boots."

"He'll have them. I'll make sure of it."

Her questioning gaze lifted to meet his.

"I want to be a part of his life," he said, looking up into her pretty green eyes. *Of* your *life*, he couldn't quite bring himself to say. "Distance isn't going to change that. He's my namesake. He should have boots and a cowboy hat."

"And apparently a razor," she said, making Garrett chuckle. Then her expression grew serious. "You are going to make a wonderful father someday."

Reaching up, he caressed her cheek. "And you have given that little boy of yours the most loving mother a child could ever ask for."

"Garrett," she said, their gazes locking. Then the baby stirred and let out a soft coo. Hannah straightened. "I… I can't wait for your entire family to meet him."

He wasn't sure what had just happened there, but it was clear Hannah had felt it, too. "They already have," he said. "The very first day he came into this world."

"That was different," she replied, her gaze lifting to meet his. "And not all of your family was there the day Austin was born."

No, they hadn't been. His father had been home watching over Blue during all the excitement. "Be forewarned," he said. "Blue is beyond excited to meet Austin. She's already planning the tea parties they can have together, and even asked Tucker to hang a baby swing from the tree next to hers so they can swing together."

A worried frown settled over Hannah's face. "Doesn't she know Austin and I will be leaving soon?"

"Blue knows what is supposed to happen," he said. "But she's hoping Austin will change his mind about leaving once he sees all the horses at the ranch."

"Oh, dear."

"It's not just Blue wanting you to stay," he said with a grin. He thought back to the nightly family dinners his mother had prepared instead of the usual once or twice a week gathering. He guessed it had been done for Hannah's sake, his mother wanted her to feel included, as well as supported, having none of her own family there for her during her stay. His brothers constantly brought up all of Hannah's wonderful qualities, as if he hadn't seen them for himself. And Autumn, well, she adored Hannah. He adored Hannah for that matter. Admired her. Wanted to kiss her.

"No?" she said, looking up at him.

It took a moment to be certain he hadn't stated his last thought aloud and wasn't rejecting him. "Uh, no. My family isn't going to want to let you leave when the time comes either. They've grown quite fond of you."

She lowered her gaze, but not before he saw a hint of disappointment in her eyes. "I've grown quite fond of your family as well. They've been so good to me during my stay."

While Garrett had enjoyed those dinners with everyone gathered around the family table, laughing and sharing bits and pieces of their day, he looked forward most to the time he was able to spend alone with Hannah during their drives back and forth to the hospital. Hours spent bonding with her son, and then sharing small talk when they'd taken breaks to grab something from the cafeteria or walked the halls.

"I'll miss having you around," he admitted.

Hannah looked up, a smile softening her face. "I'll miss you, too."

"I'm sorry to interrupt," Jessica said as she

came up to stand next to Hannah, "but it's time for me to return Austin to his crib. I need to check his vitals and then we need to run a few tests."

"Tests?" Hannah said worriedly. "Is something wrong?"

Garrett wondered the same thing. No one had said anything to them about new medical concerns where Hannah's son was concerned, and they'd been there all morning.

"Nothing's wrong," the young nurse quickly assured them.

"Thank the Lord," Hannah breathed in relief.

"The tests show us how much your son has progressed. They will also show us where Austin's lung function is and give us a better idea of when his oxygen tube can be removed. If your son continues to progress the way he is, he could be ready to go home in another couple of weeks or less."

A couple of weeks or less. A clock ticked loudly in the back of Garrett's mind. Time was running out. He needed more, but not when that could only happen if Austin's health required it.

Hannah's face lit with the news and her spring-green eyes filled with tears. She looked to Garrett. "We had better leave Jessica to her work, so they can run their tests and we'll pray for good news."

"I'll continue to keep Austin in my prayers as well," Jessica told her. "I know how hard it is to be without your baby."

"Thank you," Hannah said, the words catching in her throat.

"Yes, thank you," Garrett said, nodding. "Not only for remembering Austin in your prayers, but for watching over him when you're here and we're not."

"It's my job to see to his care," Jessica said humbly.

"It's more than that," Garrett told her. "You've been a great source of support for Hannah during this time, over and above the nursing duties you're required to perform as part of your job."

"I know I'm not supposed to get emotionally involved," she said with a hint of a frown, "but it's hard not to. I've been where Hannah is. I know the mountain she's about to climb alone as a single mother. Any words of advice I can offer her, I will gladly do so. She has my number."

"You are my inspiration," Hannah told her. "And when times get tough, which I have no doubt they will on occasion, I'll think of you."

This time it was Jessica's eyes tearing up. "Don't get me crying," she said as she reached out to take Austin from Hannah, carefully maneuvering the tubes and wires so they wouldn't catch on anything as she did so. "I can't have my vision all tear-blurred while I'm working."

Hannah stood and bent to place a tender kiss on the smattering of strawberry blonde hair covering her son's head. "Mommy will see you tomorrow." With a sigh of resignation, she stepped back.

Garrett moved in, running the side of a finger along the baby's soft cheek. "See you tomorrow, little man. Be good for your nurse."

Jessica smiled. "He always is."

Placing a hand at the small of Hannah's back, they made their way out of the neonatal intensive care unit. "Austin really is filling out," Garrett commented as they walked down the long, sterile hospital corridor.

"He is," Hannah replied happily. "It won't be long before we can finally take him home."

Before we can finally take him home. While that was not what she had meant, Garrett had images of Hannah and her son coming home to his house. Of what it might be like if the three of them truly were a family. His family. He shook his head, pushing the thought away.

They walked in companionable silence the remainder of the way through the hospital. When they reached the oversize revolving doors at the building's entrance, Garrett motioned for Hannah to step in first, and then followed her inside as it turned.

"Favorite flower," Hannah said as they stepped out onto the sidewalk.

Garrett snapped out of his reverie to find Hannah glancing over at him with a grin. "What?"

"Think fast," she said, smiling. It was a game they had begun playing to help fill the long hours they spent at the hospital. Throwing out random questions when the other wasn't expecting it. She repeated herself, and then added, "Which is your favorite? Or maybe you don't know the names of any flowers, your being a rugged cowboy and all."

His lifted a brow, and not because of the question she had asked. She clearly assumed that a cowboylike him wouldn't be able to answer that particular impromptu question. "I'll have you know I'm pretty knowledgeable when it comes to flowers."

Surprise lit her features. "You are?"

"Blue is big on going flower picking," he admitted with a grin as they crossed the parking lot. "As her uncle, it's my job to know which flowers are which."

Hannah lifted a slender brow. "I have to admit I'm impressed."

"And to answer your question," he said as they neared his truck, "A marigold."

She looked up at him. "A marigold?"

Reaching out, he opened the passenger door and helped Hannah up inside. "Yep." His grin widened. "Seems I'm a bit partial to flowers that remind me of you. Dark red marigolds that have shades of yellows and golds mixed in make me think of your hair when you're standing outside, surrounded by sunshine," he said as he closed the passenger side door and walked away with a grin.

Garrett strode from the barn, peeling off his work gloves as he went. It had been nearly a week since he'd told Hannah he liked marigolds, because they reminded him of her. The memory of it made him smile. And while the past couple of weeks had been challenging, fitting in trips to the hospital with Hannah, scheduled vet visits and tasks he needed to see to at the ranch, he was making it work—for her. Even if it meant dropping into bed dog-tired each night. Hannah would be leaving soon, and he wanted to spend as much time with her as possible before that happened. And it had nothing to do with her sunset-colored hair or her big, beautiful green eyes. Well, not completely. He liked her. All of her—from the inside out.

"Perfect timing."

He glanced up to find the woman filling his

thoughts walking toward him. Garrett smiled. "Did you rest up like you were supposed to?"

"Yes," she answered with a smile. "Did you get done whatever it was you needed to do while I rested?"

"I did. I've finished with preparations for tomorrow's vaccinations."

Hannah's gaze drifted past him to the corral beside the barn.

Garrett knew without looking what had drawn her attention in that direction. He'd just left Tucker, who was in the midst of breaking in another horse.

"What's he doing?" Hannah asked.

He cast a glance back over his shoulder, his gaze coming to rest on his youngest brother, who stood in the middle of the corral, coaxing the gelding circling the outer edge of the corral to speed up.

"Breaking in a green horse," he explained.

"Green horse?"

"A horse that isn't ready to saddle up and ride yet. That little filly he's working with right now is young and a pretty feisty yet."

"It looks dangerous," she said worriedly.

"My brother knows what he's doing," he said. "He'll get the job done and come out of it all in one piece. I promisc." He inclined his head.

"Now come on, let's take that ride I promised you last week."

Once they were seated inside, Garrett started the engine and turned to Hannah. "Windows up or down? There's a bit of a chill in the air this afternoon."

"Down," she answered. "I want to take in the fresh air and the sounds around us."

With a nod, he lowered all the windows, and then slid open the sunroof. "You let me know if the air coming in gets to be too much."

"I will," she said as they pulled away from the house. Hannah glanced around at the outbuildings and various pastures. "So, this is all part of the family business?"

"For the most part," Garrett replied. "The ranch belonged to my father, but he added our names to the deed when we went into rodeo stock contracting. That way we could insure our business, protecting our investments from unexpected loss, such as fire, infectious diseases, natural disasters."

"Like a flood," she said.

"Like a flood."

"Dad also signed over several acres of the ranch property to each of us to build our own homes on."

"That was so generous of him," Hannah said.

"He's always been very giving, wanting the best for all of us."

"I've seen that of him," Hannah said. "Of your whole family, for that matter. Your father reminds me so much of mine. It makes me realize how blessed I was not to have children with my ex-husband. He could never be the kind of father mine was, the kind I know you could be."

Garrett looked her way. "Thank you for that. It means a lot to me." Hannah believed in him. Given the chance, he would prove her right. Having noted the sadness in her tone when she spoke about father, he said, "I know you're missing your father. I'm sorry he hasn't been able to be with you through all of this."

"It's hard," she admitted. "But we talk on the phone every night. Every day he sounds so much better. Hopefully, his doctor agrees when Dad sees him this week." Her father hadn't been responding to the antibiotics treating his bronchitis and had needed to change to a stronger one, delaying his arrival even more. It was tearing Hannah up not to be there to help care for him, but she couldn't leave Austin. Thankfully, her father had several good friends looking in on him and providing him with meals, so he wouldn't have to spend his energy cooking. And he'd sounded better the last couple of times they'd spoken, which surely was a sign of his good health finally returning. "He's praying he gets the go ahead to drive up here this coming weekend. Your mother and father have invited him to stay at the ranch whenever he gets here."

"I'll pray he gets good news this week," Garrett told her, wanting Hannah to have her family, at least what she had left of it, there with her—and her there with him.

"I'm sure Dad would appreciate that."

They drove only a short distance down the road before Garrett slowed and turned onto a pull-off. Up ahead, beyond that pasture's fencing, were the horses that had been retired from the Triple W's rodeo roster. He shut off the engine and looked to Hannah. "I want you to meet some of our veteran horses. They've retired from the rodeo life and will live the remainder of their lives out here on the ranch, eating well and spending their days in leisure."

"Sounds like a pretty nice life to have," she said with a smile. Her gaze rested on the horses gathered just beyond the fence line, grazing contentedly. "They're so beautiful."

So are you was at the tip of his tongue. Thankfully, Garrett managed to hold on tight to those words. He was supposed to be giving her a tour of the ranch, not sweet-talking her with flowery compliments. Even if they were true. She was one of the prettiest, most genuine women he'd ever had the pleasure of knowing. "Come on," he said, opening his door. "Let's go have a closer look." Garrett stepped out of the truck and then made his way around in long, hurried strides to help Hannah down. Then they walked together up to the fence.

Two of the horses stopped their idle grazing to come over and greet them, sticking their heads over the top of the fence where Garrett stood. They nosed at the front of his shirt, nearly knocking him off balance with their enthusiastic greeting.

"What are they doing?" Hannah asked with a giggle.

"Begging," he said with a chuckle.

"For what?" she asked, watching their antics.

He reached into his shirt pocket and pulled out several small cubes. "Sugar. These boys have a sweet tooth like you've never seen."

"A lot like their owners, from what I've heard," Hannah said, smiling.

"We do at that," he agreed. He reached out to run his hand along the side of one of the broncs' necks. "Jackson, Tucker and I grew up surrounded by these majestic creatures. We rode before we could walk. At least, that's how Dad tells it. Mom says otherwise."

"I love listening to your father tell stories at dinner," she told him.

"You mean you love listening to him embellish the truth," Garrett corrected with a grin.

Her smile widened. "He could tell us a story about mowing the grass and make it sound exciting."

"It's not," Garrett told her. "Believe me. I'd much rather be spending time with these horses."

"I can tell," Hannah said, looking up at the mare with a smile. Sighing softly, she said, "If I hadn't just had a baby, I'd ask you to take me for a ride. I've never been on a horse before and I'd trust you to keep me safe."

He'd like to keep her, not only safe, but in his life for good. He could teach her to ride, and she could teach him to enjoy the little things in life a little more. "Someday, I will. Austin, too." Promise made, he inclined his head toward his truck. "We'd best move on. There's a lot to see."

They returned to the truck and headed farther down the road. "How did you get into contracting horses to rodeos?"

He answered, eyes still fixed on the road ahead. "After talking our thoughts over with Dad, my brothers and I decided it was what we wanted to invest our time and money into. It gave us a way to stay connected to the rodeo after we had all finally stopped competing in it. We started out contracting to supply stock to smaller, local rodeos, and, as the number in our herd grew, so did the opportunities for us to contract with even bigger rodeos. The only thing holding us back from supplying stock to the largest rodeos was the fact that we couldn't offer bulls in addition to our broncs."

"Why would you have to do that? You're horse ranchers."

"To provide for most associations, a stock contracting firm has to buy a membership and there are a lot of requirements we have to meet," he explained.

"That's a lot of hoops to jump through," she noted.

"Hoops we're more than willing to jump through," he said.

"But I thought this was a horse ranch," she said, glancing around. "I haven't seen a single bull since I've been staying here."

"It is," he said with a nod. "And you wouldn't have. We don't own any bulls. But Kade Owens does. To meet the mandatory requirements, we formed a partnership with him."

"Who is Kade Owens?"

"A good friend from our rodeo days," he explained. "Kade and Jackson competed against each other in the bull riding events before an injury ended my brother's rodeo career."

"Is that the reason for Jackson's limp?" she asked as she stood looking out over the pasture.

Garrett looked to her in surprise. "You noticed that?"

"I'm a physical therapist," she reminded him, something they had touched upon a few times during their many hospital talks. That she had taken a leave of absence after her sister and brother-in-law's passing and planned to follow that up with the allowed maternity leave after the baby was born. Her sister and Brian's will, drawn up well before Hannah had agreed to carry their child for them, had left everything to her, so she was blessed with the financially stability to stay home with Austin for a while if she chose to. And right now there was no other option. Her son needed her, and she needed him.

"I suppose that means you would be able to pick up on things others might overlook, or not give much thought to. Where Tucker and I rode mostly horses in rodeo competitions, Jackson rode bulls. The bigger the bull, the meaner the bull, the more eager he was to climb on top of it and make the ride."

"That had to be so scary."

"The rush of adrenaline that comes with taking on a sixteen or seventeen-hundred-pound bull tends to push any rational fear aside for those few short seconds. When it's man against beast. Will against will. Sometimes the bull wins," he told her. "Like it did the day Little

Shamrock, who was anything but little, won, and Jackson took a loss he couldn't come back from."

"What happened?" she asked almost hesitantly.

"A little over eight years ago, my brother was competing in the National Finals Rodeo in Las Vegas. He was riding the best he'd ever done. Made his way up to the top ten. But when the next day's competition came, Jackson seemed to be out of sorts. I'm not sure what happened to make him lose his mental focus to that extent, but it cost him, not only a lot of money, it nearly cost him his life when he was thrown by the bull he'd drawn to ride."

Hannah gasped, her hand flying up to cover her mouth.

"He landed hard and was too dazed to react before Little Shamrock trampled him."

"I thought they had clowns to chase the bull away when a rider falls," she said.

"Rodeo clowns do their best to keep the fallen riders safe, but sometimes there isn't enough time to get to the rider and to distract the bull before the damage is done. Jackson's leg sustained most of the damage, requiring a good bit of hardware to put it back together."

She groaned, as if imagining his brother's pain. "And therapy, I would imagine, with a break that severe."

"And therapy," he acknowledged with a nod.

"Your poor brother. That had to be such a hard recovery for him."

"More than we ever imagined it would be. It was as if something inside of him was broken, too, and we didn't know how to fix it." He shrugged. "Maybe it was his having been forced to accept the probability that he would never compete again. Or if he did, knowing it wouldn't be at the level he had been."

An empathetic frown pulled at her lips. "That would have to play not only on his heart, but on his mind and his pride as well."

"It did. He was angry a lot of the time in the beginning, convinced he would never be the man he was because of that almost nonexistent limp."

"Nearly nonexistent to you and me," she said, "but in Jackson's mind it's what people notice first, maybe even judge him by. I know because I've provided physical therapy for a few rodeo cowboys who also sustained rather substantial injuries."

"It changes everything for them. Even the slightest impairment can throw off a rider's ability to hold on during the ride. Depending on the kind of injury they sustained, it could affect their grip strength, balance, even the rider's ease of motion during a rough ride, as it had Jackson."

She nodded. "That makes sense. Thank the Lord he wasn't injured worse in that fall."

"I do," he admitted. "Every day. Running this business has brought us even closer than we were before. I don't know what I would do without my brothers." The thought was out before he'd processed what his words might do to Hannah, who had lost her only sibling. "I'm sorry. That was thoughtless of me."

"Don't apologize," she said with a forgiving smile. "You should feel that way. And I pray you never have to find out. At least, not for a very, very long time."

He prayed for the same thing.

"I'm glad you were the one to find me that day," Hannah said, looking up at him with an expression he couldn't quite read.

"So am I."

As if finding herself caught up in something she wasn't prepared for, a feeling he could relate to, Hannah looked away.

They drove a short distance down the road before he turned onto the dirt and gravel drive that led to his place. He'd meant what he'd told her. While he wished that Hannah had never had to go through that terrifying ordeal with the flood, and then unexpected arrival of her baby, he truly was glad that he had been the one the good Lord chose to save her. To save them. To have the honor of caring for them in their time of need.

"Your place?" she asked as they neared the house.

He nodded. "I want to show you my veterinary clinic. Not that I use it much. Except for storing medications and supplies, most of my work is done out in fields and barns, since I deal mainly in the care of large animals. Horse, cows, etcetera."

"What about smaller animals like cats and dogs?"

"There's a vet in town who handles domesticated animals," he explained. "We fill in for each other when needed."

He pulled up in front of the building that served as his clinic and cut the engine. "Now sit tight until I come around to help you down."

"Garrett, I'm perfectly capable of getting out of your truck on my own," Hannah said, reaching for the door handle.

"I prefer to help you down because this truck is higher up than most," he explained. "And if you were to fall getting out, my mother would have my head. The rest of my family probably would as well. I happen to like my head where it sits, atop my shoulders, so please just sit there until I come around."

Hannah laughed softly. "Well, when you put it that way."

After helping her down, Garrett walked her to the office entrance. He unlocked the door and then eased it open. "After you," he said.

She stepped inside, her gaze moving slowly about the room. "It looks almost like a doctor's office," she noted. "Except for the skeletal posters of animals hanging on the wall behind the examination bed."

Before Garrett could respond, his cell phone rang. "I'm sorry," he said, apologizing for the interruption. He pulled out his phone and glanced down at the screen, then back up at Hannah. "Work call. Do you mind if I step outside and take this?"

"Take your call," she said. "I'll be fine."

With a nod, he left and closed the door behind him.

Hannah turned to find the wall opposite to the one with all the posters on it filled with framed pictures. Most of them were of horses. Probably, if she had to guess, horses Garrett had either owned, still owned or had ridden in competition. It made her smile. The room was filled with the things that made him the happiest: his family and his horses.

She walked over to take a closer look at the

photos. There were several of Garrett and his brothers, which looked to have been taken at various rodeos. A much larger family portrait hung in the center of the wall, one that looked to have been taken maybe ten years or so earlier. Emma had no streaks of silver in her coppery hair, and her sons had smooth, whisker-free faces with youthful grins, the spitting images of their father, who stood, beaming with pride, alongside his family.

A lone frame, one much smaller than the ones on the wall sat next to a mission-style lamp atop a table by the window. Hannah walked over, thinking it to be Autumn because of the woman's lighter hair. But when she drew close enough to see the fine details of the photograph, she saw that it wasn't a woman, but a girl probably about sixteen or so, with long, blond hair and a sweet smile.

Lifting the framed photo, she studied it closer. The girl was too old to be the daughter Emma and Grady had lost years before. It took only a moment longer for the realization to strike her. This was Grace. The girl Garrett had given his whole heart to.

A mix of emotions washed over her at that moment. Sadness for the beautiful, young girl who'd fought so hard to live and hadn't. And shame, for feeling even the slightest bit of envy toward Grace because she had been so loved by Garrett. The depth of which Hannah had never known from her husband during their brief marriage.

The office door opened, and Hannah fumbled to return the picture to its place on the table. Then she spun around with a forced smile. "All done with your call?"

Garrett stood silent in the doorway, his gaze moving past her to the picture no longer sitting where it had been. Hannah felt as if she'd been caught doing something she shouldn't have. But it wasn't anger that filled his eyes as he crossed the room to stand beside her. It was pain. "Her name was Grace," he said, looking down at the photo.

"I know," she said softly.

His gaze snapped up to meet hers. "How? Did one of my brothers say something to you about her? Because it wasn't their place to do so."

"Autumn told me," she admitted.

"Autumn?" he said. "I suppose I shouldn't be surprised that she knew about Grace. There are no secrets between my brother and his wife. As it should be," he conceded. "But why would she feel the need to share my past with you?"

"Please don't be angry with her," Hannah said, regret knotting up in her stomach. She hadn't wanted to betray her new friend, but she couldn't lie to Garrett either. "Autumn wants you and Jackson to find the same kind of happiness she and Tucker have found."

"And that's going to happen by her bringing up my past?" he asked stiffly.

"I don't think she would have said anything about it if I hadn't pressed her for the reason you and Jackson are so guarded with your hearts. I, for one, couldn't imagine any woman wanting to break your heart. You're one of the best men I've ever known. I had no idea the loss you had experienced had been so final." A love he had carried with him all those years. Hannah couldn't help but wonder what it would be like to be loved so deeply by a man. By Garrett.

When no response came, Hannah went on, "I know I shouldn't have asked. It wasn't any of my business. But I care about you, Garrett. I want more than anything for you to be happy."

"I can't promise that I'll ever open myself up to the kind of happiness you and Autumn want for me. And I'm good with that. It's better than loving and... It's just better," he said, his voice raspy with emotion.

Her eyes filled with tears as Hannah reached up to tenderly place a hand on his tanned cheek. "Oh, Garrett," she said sadly. "What it must have cost you to step foot into that hospital with me on that rainy day, and all the days since…" Her words trailed off.

"To be honest," he said, his hand covering the one she had place against his cheek, "my past wasn't what was front and foremost in my mind the second I stepped into the emergency room with you and your newborn son. All I knew was that I would not lose you, too, either of you, after promising you that everything would be all right."

"Is that what happened with Grace?"

He looked to Grace's picture. "Yes. That's why I keep her picture there. As a reminder."

"As a reminder of what?" she asked, searching his face.

He closed his eyes. "Of the lie I told her. Her father had taken me aside to tell me that she was dying, and to ask me to pray for her to find peace from her suffering. I couldn't bring myself to pray. I was too angry at God for wanting to take Grace from us. Instead, I went into her hospital room to see her and told her that she was going to be okay. And then she died."

"You didn't lie to her," Hannah told him, her heart aching for all that he had gone through. Watching his first love fade away, day by day, as the life slipped from her weakened body, knowing Grace had no more strength left in her to fight, and he would be there for her until the end.

Garrett opened his eyes to reveal the moisture that had gathered there. "I told her everything would be okay. *She* would be okay."

"And she is," Hannah said. "She is in a far better place than any of us. She's no longer suffering. If you did anything, you gave Grace comfort when she needed it most. Because that's the kind of man you are. I should know."

To her surprise, Garrett drew her to him, hugging her tight. "Thank you, Hannah. You have been one of the biggest blessings in my life."

She hugged him back, a tear slipping out to run down her cheek. "As you have been for me."

Chapter Eight

Hannah's heart skittered, as it always seemed to do whenever Garrett appeared. She watched as he rode toward the house the next day. The man sat as if he'd been born in the saddle, which, she supposed, he pretty much had been.

"Morning," she greeted as he drew back on the reins, stopping next to the porch where Hannah was enjoying a cup of warm cider.

"Morning," he replied, giving his cowboy hat a nudge. "I was on my way to help Jackson and Tucker clear away some of the storm debris that's plugging up part of the creek and noticed you sitting out here on the porch. Figured I'd swing by and say hello."

"I'm glad you did." She found herself imagining what it would be like to be married to Garrett, waiting on their own porch to welcome her husband home every day. The image seemed so clear in her mind, unlike something her wishful thinking might have conjured up.

He looked toward the house. "Mom and Dad up yet?"

"I don't think so," she said, shaking her head.

"Ah, the benefits of retirement." He rounded the porch and ascended the steps. "You're up earlier than usual, aren't you?"

"A little. I wanted to see the sunrise," she admitted with a smile. "And I have to say it didn't disappoint. The warm, vibrant shades of red and gold the rising sun casts across the land and distant mountains are beyond breathtaking."

"You should see it in the deep of winter," he told her. "When the colors of dawn glisten off the freshly fallen snow." He raised up in the saddle and then swung his leg over the back of his horse, before dropping to the ground below. "So is that the only reason you're up this early?" he asked as he wrapped his horse's reins around the railing and then stepped up onto the porch.

She smiled up at him from the chair she was seated in. "Are you implying that I was sitting out here watching for you?" And how close to the truth that would be.

"Can't blame a man for doing a little wishful thinking," he replied with a teasing grin as he settled into the white wicker porch chair next to hers.

Hannah looked out across the yard. "I might have been hoping for a glimpse of you riding up to the barn." She didn't have to see Garrett's face to know that his smile widened with her admission. "Or," she continued, shifting her attention back to the cowboy beside her, "I might have been hoping to catch a glimpse of that very handsome horse of yours."

"Something tells me I'm not going to find out which it is."

She laughed. "You're probably right."

"Maybe I can weaken your resolve by using my cowboy charm on you," he said with a playful wriggle of his brows.

Hannah laughed softly, despite the butterflies his words had set to fluttering in her stomach. "Now you're not fighting fair." She leaned her head back against the wicker chair. "What I'd really like is to know more about you and your family."

He stretched out his long, denim-clad legs as he eased back in the chair next to hers and tucked his hands behind his head. "Ask away."

She liked that about Garrett. He was always so honest and open with her. "Jackson left the rodeo because of his injury," she began.

Garrett nodded.

"Was it the same for you and Tucker? Injuries forcing you out?"

"No," he said, shaking his head. "He and I left on our own terms. Truth is, Tucker sort of lost his spark for competing on the circuit after his marriage to Autumn's sister fell apart. Not that anyone realized why at the time since he kept his marriage from us. But looking back, knowing what we do now, it all makes sense. I think his focus was consumed by questions he had no answers to, and a loss of focus when riding can be dangerous for both the rider and the animal."

"I can only imagine."

"Would you mind my asking about your sister? That is, unless it's too hard for you to talk about her."

"I don't mind," she told him. She didn't want to set her memories of her sister aside. Being able to talk about them, even though it could be hard emotionally, kept her sister alive in her heart. "Heather was older than me, but only by two years, so we were pretty close. She was the athlete in our family, running track, even in college. I was more gifted on the academic side. Not that I didn't like sports. I played tennis and I liked to swim, just not competitively."

"Unlike my brothers and myself, who lived for the competition," he said with a grin.

"There are times I find myself reaching for the phone to call her," she admitted with a frown.

"I'm sure you do," he said. "She hasn't been gone that long."

Not long, but far too long. "What about you? What made you decide to retire from riding," she asked, her gazed now fixed on him.

"My career," he answered. "I didn't ride at the same competitive level my brothers did, entering only local rodeos while pursuing my degree in veterinary medicine. After graduation, when I opened my own practice, I gave it up altogether."

"Too busy with work?"

"Too concerned I might not be able to work," he told her. "The possibility of getting bucked and breaking an arm wasn't a risk I was willing to take. I'd worked too long, and too hard, to get my degree to throw it all away. I was done. Or so I'd thought. But then I ended up following the rodeo circuit anyway when my brothers and I went into the rodeo stock contracting business, Tucker and Jackson training the horses, and me seeing to any medical issues that might arise with the horses here at the ranch or when we are attending scheduled rodeos."

"I'd imagine it's a big plus to have an on-site vet."

"It definitely saves us money," he agreed.

"Your parents have to be so proud of what you and your brothers have accomplished," Hannah said with a soft smile.

"They are," Garrett said, his parents having told them as much more times than he could count. "I still wish we could've talked Dad into joining us in our venture, but he wanted to spend his golden years focusing on Mom and their life together."

"That's so romantic," she sighed, wondering if she would ever be so blessed as to have the kind of life, the kind of love, that her parents and Garrett's parents had shared. Would Garrett ever want that for himself?

He chuckled. "I suppose so."

"It is," she insisted, laughing softly.

"I'm not sure romance had anything to do with it," Garrett said. "I think it was more Dad's way of doing the right thing. Mom stood by him during all the years he rode rodeo, supporting him completely. When he retired, he decided it was his turn to do for her. Not that he doesn't lend a hand when we need it. For example, he'll be going on the road this rodeo season to cover for Tucker who will be staying in Bent Creek to care for Blue and oversee things here at the ranch."

"And your mom's okay with his leaving?"

"She'll be going with him," Garrett explained. "My parents recently purchased an RV to take trips in, so they'll be able to travel together while lending Jackson and myself a hand at the different rodeos we've contracted for this coming season. Mom can't wait to hit the road again. The only thing giving her hesitation is the thought of being away from Blue for so long, but Tucker and Autumn are going to try to bring Blue to a rodeo or two, which helped ease Mom's guilt over leaving her new granddaughter for most of the summer."

"Who will see to the ranch when everyone's gone?"

"We have part-time ranch hands who we trust to see to things while we're all away." He looked to her in surprise. "You know, I have to admit I never expected to be having this conversation with you."

"Why ever not?"

"You said yourself that you had never been to a rodeo," he explained. "I didn't think the aspects of my family's business would really interest you."

"I may never have been to any shows," she said, "but that doesn't mean I wouldn't want to go to one. The opportunity just never arose for me to do so."

Her words took him by surprise. "You'd like to go to a rodeo?"

"Yes. Not that it's going to happen anytime in the near future," Hannah said, looking off toward the distant mountains. "But after hearing so much about it from you and your family, my interest is most definitely piqued. Maybe when Austin is older we can go to one."

"I'm sure he'll like that," he said, hating the thought of her having to go it alone when it came to raising her son. "My brothers and I grew up going to rodeos. Dad competed in them until I was twelve or so, so we'd go to watch him."

"That had to be so exciting."

He nodded with a grin as he recalled the special times he'd shared with his family. Times that he as a young boy had taken for granted.

"It was," Garrett replied. "My brothers and I used to love watching Dad ride. We couldn't wait until we were old enough to sit atop a bucking horse ourselves, or in Jackson's case a bucking bull, and compete. Not that Dad didn't get us involved in other activities when we were growing up, like fishing and camping."

Hannah looked his way, something bordering on panic etched in her pretty face. "Garrett, I don't know how to fish or build a campfire. Or any of those things dads usually do with their sons."

"There is no set rule saying all boys have to know how to fish or set up camp," he told her, wanting to ease some of Hannah's worry. She had enough on her mind as it was.

"But most boys do," she argued, fretting her lower lip.

Most did where he was from, but that was the norm in the area he had grown up in. "I could teach him." The offer was out before he considered the impossibility of it. They would be living in two different states.

"You?" she said, some of that sparkle coming back into those beautiful green eyes of hers.

He should have rescinded his offer with an apology for getting her hopes up, reminding her of their geographical differences. He should have suggested that Austin wouldn't be ready for fishing or camping for several more years yet, and that by then she would probably have someone special in her life. A man who would appreciate the wonderful, loving woman she was. A man willing to step in for the father Austin had so tragically lost and give Hannah more children. The ones she'd been denied in her first marriage.

"If you'd like," he said instead, promptly shoving aside any thought of the man Hannah would someday give her heart to. And her smile. And her precious son. The boy she'd so trustingly placed in his arms right after he'd come into this world. It shouldn't bother him, Garrett thought, guilt jabbing at his gut. If anything, he should pray for the Lord to grant her the happiness she deserved. But the problem was *he* wanted to be the man to give her that happiness.

"I can't think of anyone I feel more comfortable with than you when it comes to being there for my son. But I can't ask that of you."

His smile sagged. "Why not?"

"Because that time is years away," she explained. "You'll be busy with a family of your own by the time Austin is ready to learn all of those things."

He shook his head. "Marriage isn't in my future."

She reached out, covering his hand with hers, saying softly, "Because of Grace?"

"That's part of it," he said, his gaze on their joined hands.

"You don't want children?" she asked, her expression troubled.

He hesitated a long moment before answering. "I'm not able to have children," he admitted. "That's pretty much what marriages are for."

"Garrett," Hannah gasped, her hand tightening over his. "I'm so sorry. I had no idea."

"You wouldn't," he said soberly. "It's not something I've felt the need to share with others."

"But you're telling me."

He cleared his throat, which suddenly felt constricted. "I'm telling you because you've shared so many confidences with me." And because he trusted her. "I hope it will help you will understand a little better why marriage isn't in my future."

"Marriage isn't only about creating a family," she told him with a frown. "It's about finding that one special person to love and be loved by. It's about supporting each other through the good and the bad. It's about trust and commitment. It's about sharing a faith and allowing that faith to guide you through your lives together."

"How can you feel so strongly about marriage?" he asked her. "After what happened with your first."

"Because forever is a very long time to spend alone."

"You'll have Austin."

She nodded. "I will. But I pray for the Lord to bring someone into my life to complete our family."

"You deserve that," he said solemnly.

"Garrett…" she asked hesitantly "…are you certain you can't have children?"

"According to the doctors who treated me following the bronc riding injury that sent me to the emergency room in Missouri the year before I gave up competitive riding for good, I am. And I only have myself to blame for it."

"You were a competitive bronc rider," she told

him. "That meant risking possible injury each and every time you rode. But accidents can happen in any line of work. You shouldn't blame yourself for what happened."

"It could have been prevented," came his muttered admission.

She looked up at him. "What do you mean?"

"My sterility could have been prevented." His frown deepened. "I put off going to the ER after my ride, even though I was in a great deal of pain, because of my aversion to hospitals after losing Grace. If I had sought medical attention right away, sterility would probably not have been an issue." He laughed, the sound almost brittle. "The rodeo left its mark on all of us. Jackson with his lame leg. Tucker's broken marriage. And my infertility. The funny thing is, despite all of that, we still love being a part of the rodeo circuit."

Moisture filled her eyes as she sat looking up at him.

"Hannah, please don't cry."

"I can't help it," she said as her tears swelled in her eyes. "When I think of all my coming here has cost you emotionally. Having you hold Austin so I could rest after giving birth to him. That had to be so hard for you. If I had known…"

"I would have held him anyway," he told her with a tender smile. "You needed to get some sleep. And I promise my thoughts weren't on anything but the unexpected little blessing I was holding in my arms at that moment."

"But then you drove Austin and me to the hospital. To the place that holds your last memories of Grace. Painful memories. And it didn't end there. You spent hours on end on a floor filled with newborns when you can't…" She didn't finish what she'd been about to say.

It had cost him emotionally. He couldn't deny it. But it was nothing compared to what it had gained him. "That first day," he began, "when I brought you and Austin in through those emergency room doors, my main focus was on getting you and your son the medical help you both needed." His gaze locked with hers. "I wasn't going to lose you. Either of you. And while I'll admit it's been hard, I found myself wanting to be there for you in the days following Austin's birth more than I wanted to avoid memories from my past."

"Garrett," she said with a tender, teary-eyed smile.

"It's true," he said. "You've given me new memories where that hospital is concerned. So if anyone should be doing the thanking, it should be me. You've helped me to let go of some of the past that I should have let go of a long time ago."

Tears spilled out onto her cheeks. "How can I

ever thank you for the emotional sacrifice you've made for us? Are still making," she added with a soft sob.

Garrett turned his hand over, threading his fingers through hers. "By being happy."

Nodding, she brushed a tear from her cheek with a soft sniffle. "I want the same for you. And whether or not you can father a child makes you no less lovable. Plenty of couples adopt."

He frowned. "Maybe so, but I would always wonder if any woman I would marry would start to resent having to raise someone else's child when they could have had one of their own."

"If you were my husband, would you feel that way about raising Austin?" she asked, making him take a mental step back. "Because he's my sister's son, not mine. Just as he won't be a physical part of any man I might marry. Should I avoid ever marrying again because my husband might resent, if not me, then the child I will be raising as my son?"

The last thing he wanted to think about was the man who would be part of Hannah's future. But her bringing it up made him rethink his thoughts on the matter. "No," he muttered. "*If* I were your husband, I would love you even more for opening your heart and giving a motherless child a special place in your heart. And I would love Austin. I can't imagine any man not wanting to be a father to your son." But to be that meant that man would be more than just a father to Austin. He'd be Hannah's husband and all the things Garrett found himself wanting, despite knowing they were just out of reach.

"I pray you're right," she said with a soft sigh. Looking his way, she asked, "Do you have time to go for a short walk? I'd like to stretch my legs a bit."

He managed a smile. "For you? Always." Reaching out, he took hold of her hand.

Hannah glanced down at their joined hands, her heart dancing happily as he walked her across the porch. She felt like a young girl on a first date, rather than a grown woman simply spending time with a friend. Because that's what Garrett was to her—a very dear friend. Someone she could share her innermost feelings with, with the exception of those she held for him. Something that had been missing from her life since losing her sister.

"Will you tell me a little more about the ranch and your rodeo business?"

"What would you like to know?" he asked as they walked along.

"How big is your ranch?"

"Eight thousand acres in total," he replied.

"That's huge." She looked around, her gaze coming to rest on the herd of broncs grazing in the distance. "But then you probably need that much land for all the horses you have."

"They're our livelihood," he explained. "They need room to roam."

"How many horses live on your ranch?"

He followed the line of her gaze. "We have 110 rodeo-ready horses, foals that have yet to come into their own, about a dozen or so retired broncs. That's not counting our own personal saddle horses." He pointed to the barn. "We store supplies and feed for our stock horses in the main barn."

They moved past the barn to where a pair of double-decker semitrucks were parked next to one of the galvanized grain bins. "Horse trailers?" Hannah inquired as she took in the sight of them. They looked newer and had fancy, scrolled detailing around their doors, a saddle painted on each side of the elongated horse trailers with Triple W Rodeo Ranch arched over the top.

Garrett nodded. "We use these for equine transport to the various rodeos. They are top-of-the-line with every safety measure and comfort taken into consideration. We want to be certain our horses make it to their contracted destinations safely, experiencing as little stress as possible."

"Wow. So much goes into operating a stock contracting company," Hannah said in awe.

"This," she said, motioning to everything around her, "is all so impressive, Garrett. And to think I had only pictured a rodeo consisting of a fenced-in riding area with a gate for riders to come in and out of, and a bunch of horse trailers. But there is so much more to it."

Garrett chuckled. "A lot more than in your imaginings from the sounds of it. You really need to experience the real thing."

"I know," she said with a wistful sigh as she stared off toward the herd galloping across the pasture beyond the barn.

"How about this evening?"

She looked his way, her questioning gaze meeting his. "What?"

"There's a local rodeo this evening over in Shanter," he said of the town thirty-five minutes away from Bent Creek, even closer from the hospital they drove to every day. "It's an indoor competition, one that's a somewhat scaled-down version of the rodeos our company normally contracts for, but it's a rodeo all the same. I was thinking that if you are feeling up to it after visiting with Austin today, we can take a ride over and check it out."

Her face lit up instantly at his suggestion, snagging yet another piece of Garrett's heart.

"We can even grab some dinner there if you're good with burgers."

"You already had me sold on the idea, but burgers totally sealed the deal."

"It's a date then," Garrett said without thinking. Then frowned at his words. "Well, not a date exactly. You know what I mean."

Her smile sagged ever so slightly. And then she laughed, sounding forced. "Of course. I've just had a baby. Not what most men are looking for when it comes to dating."

His brows drew together. "It has nothing to do with your son. If things were different," he told her, regret filling him, "I would ask you out in a heartbeat. I like you, Hannah. I like you a lot. But you deserve a man who can give you children. A man who can give Austin brothers and sisters." He looked around, feeling uneasy with the direction their conversation had taken. The last thing he wanted to do was lay his heart out there on the line when doing so wouldn't change anything. "I should be going. I'm supposed to help Tucker and Jackson clean some of the storm debris out of the creek before it damns up."

"Thank you for taking the time to walk with me this morning."

He nodded. "I'll be back to pick you up around three." Walking over to his horse, Garrett unwound the reins from where he'd secured them to the porch railing, and then swung up into the saddle.

"Garrett…" Hannah said as he turned his horse to leave. "You never did ask what my favorite flower is."

He cast a curious glance her way.

"A while ago, I asked what yours was," she explained. "You told me a marigold. I thought you might want to know what my favorite is." She waited patiently for him to ask.

Unable to help himself, Garrett smiled. He'd wanted a change in conversation. This was definitely it. "All right, Hannah, what is your favorite flower?"

Her lips drew up into a bright smile. "That's easy. A sunflower."

As her reply settled in, Hannah moved up onto the porch.

"A sunflower, huh?" he repeated. "Not a perfectly bloomed rose or brightly colored tulip,"

"Nope. Definitely a sunflower," she replied. Reaching for the screen door, she glanced back at him over her slender shoulder. "They're tall and I like tall. And strong. Always tipping their faces upward to soak in the warmth of the sun. Mostly because they remind me of you," she said with a playful wink. "See you after work."

The screen door swung shut behind her, leaving Garrett to process her admission. It didn't matter that she'd compared him to a flower. What mattered was that he was *her* kind of flower. Hope, as irrational as it was, stirred inside him as he rode away.

"The burgers were awesome, but these are the best fries ever," Hannah said, looking up at him with a happy grin as they made their way to their seats in the front row of the rodeo arena.

They had grabbed a couple of burgers and fries when they'd gotten to the rodeo. Garrett had finished all his, but Hannah was still enjoying the last bit of her fries. "Mine were good," he replied. "But that's because they weren't all smothered in ketchup and vinegar, like some people's." He followed that up with an exaggerated cringe.

Laughing, she held the cone-shaped paper cup out to him. "Don't knock it until you try it, cowboy."

He eyed the cup's contents warily. "Thanks, but I'm a plain fry kind of guy."

"Don't tell me a man who used to climb onto a bronc, risking life and limb, is afraid to try a little, tiny, flavor-induced French fry."

"You don't play fair," he said with a grin as he reached out to pluck a couple of fries from the cup. Then he popped them into his mouth, prepared to force them down just to prove to Hannah that he was still the fearless cowboy he'd once been. But Garrett discovered, much to his surprise, that fries were actually very tasty with ketchup and vinegar added to them. "Mmm…" he moaned.

Her smile widened. "Good, right?"

"Best fries ever," he agreed, helping himself to another one as they headed toward the arena to take their seats. There had been so many firsts for him since Hannah came into his life. First time he'd ever rescued someone. First time he'd ever held a newborn. First time he'd ever thought about how empty his life, a life filled with work and family, still was.

"Garrett?"

Garrett stopped and turned, catching sight of two men he used to compete against when he was riding the circuit. "Huck," he greeted with a nod. "Ben."

"You thinking about coming out of retirement?" Ben asked with a grin. "Here to check out the competition?"

"Not a chance." He looked to Hannah. "I'm just here with a friend."

"Well, if I had the choice of sitting atop a bronc or beside this pretty lady here, I'd definitely stay retired." Ben's words made Hannah blush.

Huck nodded in agreement.

"Hannah Wade, meet Huck Salyers and Ben Freeman," Garrett said.

Both men tipped their cowboy hats, murmuring their greetings.

"It's my first rodeo," Hannah told them. "I'm so excited to see this part of Garrett's life."

Both men slid questioning glances his way.

Not wanting to have to make explanations to soothe their curiosity, Garrett said, "I hate to cut this short, but we really need to get to our seats. The bareback bronc event is getting ready to start."

The men nodded.

"It was good seeing you," Huck said.

"Enjoy the rodeo," Ben told Hannah.

"I'm sure I will," she replied with a smile.

Garrett felt a stirring of something akin to jealousy as he stood listening to his friend make small talk with Hannah. Maybe it was because they were on the receiving end of her pretty smile. One he'd prefer to have aimed solely at him. He should have introduced Hannah as his girl, because that's what he wanted her to be— his girl. It was high time he stopped fighting it. He turned to her as the two men walked away, intending to tell her just that, but the rodeo announcer came on the speakers to announce the bareback bronc event was about to begin.

"We're going to miss the start," she fretted.

"Not if we hurry," he said, taking her hand as he led her through the thinning crowd.

She tossed her empty fry container into a nearly trash barrel as they hurried toward the bleachers that wrapped around the dirt-packed arena.

"Why are there other riders here?" she asked, sounding almost breathless with anticipation as they made their way up the steps and along the front row of bleacher seats.

"Those are the pickup men," he explained as they located their seats and settled onto them. "Their job is to see to the safety of whichever cowboy's competing at that time. At the end of the ride, or even during if there appears to be trouble, they come in and help him safely to the ground. Then they herd the horse out of the arena."

"That's comforting to know," she replied as she eyed the two men on horseback.

The rodeo announcer's voice boomed out of the overhead speakers, "This is Give Him a Shake, seeing if he can do just that to Brock Lemley from Utah." Music began to play. A second later, the chute opened. From that moment on, Hannah was riveted, at the edge of her seat as she watched the competition.

Despite the action going on inside the arena as rider after rider came out, each one trying to bring in the top score of the night, Garrett's attention kept drifting to Hannah, who was leaning forward, both hands curled tightly around the railing in front of her.

Her gaze stuck like glue to the bronc rider currently making his ride in the arena. Her wide-eyed expression, and soft, worried gasps as the bronc bucked with increased determination had Garrett wondering if Hannah was going to last the entire rodeo. The night was only beginning.

The buzzer sounded, signaling the end of the required ride, but the bronc wasn't ready to quit. Another violent buck, followed by a sharp cut to the right, sent the rider airborne.

Hannah let out a terrified shriek as the rodeo cowboy hit the ground about twenty feet away from where they sat watching, hard enough to send up a small cloud of dust. "Garrett—" her hand shot out, frantically grabbing for his "—is he okay?"

He eyed the fallen cowboy, praying that he hadn't brought Hannah to a rodeo only to have a serious injury happen right there in front of them. Thankfully, the man pushed upright, shook his head as if trying to clear the cobwebs from it, and then scrambled to his feet.

"A little dazed," Garrett supposed as he watched the rider break into a jog toward the fence, slapping his dust-covered cowboy hat against his leg as he went. "But medical will check him out."

Nodding, she watched in silence as the young rider made his way out of the arena, her hand still clutching Garrett's like a lifeline.

He liked being the one she turned to when she was afraid. Giving her hand a squeeze, he said, "You okay?"

"A little shaken," she admitted. "Are those horses always so…rough? Yours always seem so calm."

"That's because they don't have riders on them," he told her. "But these horses are bred to buck hard. That's how those cowboys want it. The rougher the ride, the better the score, as long as the rider holds on for the mandatory eight seconds. Getting bucked is a part of this sport."

"Do riders get disqualified when they're thrown?"

"Not if they're still on their bronc when the buzzer sounds," Garrett explained. "That last rider made it the eight seconds before he was thrown, and it was a hard ride. All in all, it was a pretty good one."

"Good that he didn't break his neck when he fell," Hannah muttered. "I can't believe you used to do this."

"It looks worse than it actually is," he said, wanting to set her mind at ease. "Most riders are experienced enough to know how to fall to prevent any real serious injury. Not that accidents don't happen on occasion." He and Jackson were living proof of that. "And most riders opt to wear protective vests and chaps, which help to cushion falls as well as offer an extra layer of protection between the skin and the flailing hooves of a bucking horse. Helmets and face guards have also become more commonplace with riders."

She appeared to relax with his explanation. "That's reassuring." Her gaze returned to the arena as the next rider shot out of the chute. The bronc bucked hard, with a sidestepping hop into the fence. Pain registered on the cowboy's face as he struggled to regain his balance. The second the pickup men knew the rider was in trouble, they moved in to help get him safely off the horse.

Hannah gave a quick prayer of thanks that the man had come away with little more than a limp. She turned to Garrett. "I can't believe you used to do this."

"I did," he acknowledged.

"Weren't you terrified when you climbed onto whatever horse you had to ride?"

He shrugged. "It was more of an adrenaline rush, combined with the determination to make each ride better than my last. But then I grew up around the rodeo, not to mention having two very competitive brothers who were both happy to give me a push whenever I needed it."

She bit at her bottom lip as the next rider came out of the gate.

"If this is too much for you, we can go," he told Hannah worriedly.

"We can't leave yet," she said, looking up at him. "This is the most exciting thing I've ever done, and all I'm doing is sitting here."

Her response made him smile.

"I'm glad you're enjoying yourself."

"I am," she said happily. "More than you could ever know."

If it was anywhere close to the way he felt about the time they had spent together that evening, then he did know.

Still holding hands, they watched the rodeo, Hannah never hesitating in asking questions whenever one came to mind. Her interest was genuine, and Garrett was touched that she truly wanted to learn about the world he'd grown up in. A world his life was now built around. The women he'd come across during his years on the circuit, the ones seeking to strike up something with a rodeo cowboy, the ones he hadn't been inclined to take interest in, hadn't really cared about who he was. It was all about what he was—a fairly successful rodeo cowboy. With Hannah, the connection was more genuine.

The ride back to his parents' place was filled with Hannah's excited chatter.

Garrett pulled up in front of his childhood home and shut off the engine. "I'll walk you to the door."

"You don't have to," she told him. "I know it's late and you have to get up at the crack of dawn."

"I want to." He made his way around to the passenger side where he helped Hannah down and then walked her to the porch.

Stopping at the door, she turned to look up at him. "I had so much fun this evening."

He smiled down at her. "I'm glad."

"I just wish I could've gone to a rodeo with you back when you were competing."

He found himself wishing she had been a part of his life back then, too. He liked having Hannah around. Their conversations. Her laughter. Her smiles. "You would have seen pretty much what you saw there today."

"Only it would have been *you* out there, making my heart pound," she replied.

"And here I thought it was just being with me that made women's hearts pound," he said with a teasing grin. "Looks like I'm going to have to work on my cowboy charm."

Hannah laughed softly and reached up to give the brim of his hat a playful tug. "I think between this cowboy hat, this adorable dimple," she said, her finger jabbing lightly at the divot in his cheek, "and your big heart, you have more than perfected the charm."

"Enough to convince you to go on a date with me again?" he teased.

"I thought this wasn't a real date," she said, her eyes searching his.

Garrett took a mental step back, his grin flattening. "I'm sorry, Hannah. I'm not real sure what this is." He hadn't dated since high school.

Her smile sagged, and she immediately averted her gaze elsewhere. "Don't apologize. Your inability to call it that is answer enough."

He hated that he'd hurt her feelings with his thoughtless words. "If I could be the man you deserve, which we both know I will never be, then this would have been a real date, as far as I'm concerned. The best I've ever been on," he admitted.

"It was for me, too," she said softly. "My ex-husband and I didn't go out much. He was more of a homebody. Tonight showed me what I've been missing all these years."

He reached out, cupped her chin and turned her head until she was looking up at him once more. "I'm sorry your marriage didn't work out the way you'd hoped it would."

"It wasn't meant to be," she told him. "And the Lord blessed me with the chance to carry a child. Not my own, but I was able to experience the feeling of a life growing inside of me, something I had longed for. It was wondrous. And then it was scary, having nearly lost Austin. I'm not sure I want to ever go through that again."

He let his hand fall away, his brows drawing together in surprise. "I thought you wanted a big family." They'd talked about her desire to have several children more than once during those long days spent at the hospital.

"I would very much like to have a big family someday. But there are other ways. Other children are in need of someone willing to raise and love them like they were their own. Of course, that would depend on whoever the Lord has in mind for me, and if adoption is something my husband would consider."

It was hard for Garrett to process that. But he supposed Austin's early arrival and the complications that followed had been traumatic enough to have Hannah considering adoption for her future family. Then it struck him, his sterility wouldn't come into play if Hannah preferred adoption instead of giving birth to her own children. Hope flared to life inside him.

"Hannah…" he said, trying to get a grip on all the emotions that had suddenly stirred up inside him. Happiness. Excitement. A little fear. Because this moment could change everything he had always envisioned for his future.

"Yes?"

"I think we should call this a date."

She gave a regretful shake of her head. "If things were different," she said, "and I'm not referring to having children, I would love to. But it would be too hard to start something, fall for you even more than I already have, and then have to say goodbye in a week or so, maybe less."

More than I already have. His heart began thudding against his chest with her admission. "Then don't say goodbye. Move here to Bent Creek. Give this connection between us a chance to grow." *Let me love you.* "There are plenty of hospitals and rehab facilities, even nursing homes, where you could seek employment if you decide you want to go back to work."

Her smile slid away. "If only it were that simple."

"It is," he said, despite knowing better than most that nothing in life was simple.

Hannah shook her head. "If it were only me, I'd give it some serious consideration. It's hard to live in a place where I am constantly surrounded by memories. Of Mom. Of Heather and Brian. Of the happy, loving family I once had."

He nodded in understanding, having gone through that himself after losing Grace. So many memories. Memories he suddenly realized had grown hazy since Hannah's unexpected arrival in his life.

Before he had a chance to respond, she went on, "But I have my father to think about. He needs me right now. And he needs his grandson. We're all he has left in this world. I can't take that from him, no matter how tempting the thought of building a new life in a place like Bent Creek might be." Hannah rose up on her toes and then leaned in to place a sweet kiss on his cheek. "If things were different, I would choose to stay here with you." Stepping back, she opened the door, her suddenly teary gaze meeting his. "Thank you for tonight, Garrett. It's a memory I will hold dear forever." Then she was gone, the door easing shut behind her.

Chapter Nine

"Thank you again for the omelet," Hannah said as she stood from the table to carry her plate and fork over to the sink. "It was delicious."

"I'd like to say they're my specialty," Garrett replied as he followed her with his own breakfast dishes, "but I only make omelets because I can't flip an egg without breaking its yoke."

She laughed. "Good for me you're a poor egg-flipper. I much prefer an omelet over a no-frills egg."

Garrett chuckled, despite the growing sense of panic in his gut. They had been informed the afternoon before, while visiting her son in the hospital, that they expected to release Austin that coming Tuesday. That meant he had two, maybe three days left to spend with Hannah before she walked out of his life forever.

"You wash, I'll dry," Garrett said, pulling a tea towel from the kitchen drawer.

"Sounds like a plan," Hannah said, setting their dirty dishes down into the still-sudsy water his mother had left in the sink before rushing off to church that morning.

His parents had told Hannah they had to leave early that morning to meet with a few of their church parishioners. It wasn't a lie, because they were joining his brothers, Autumn and a few of his mother's friends, all members of their church, at Garrett's place where they were setting up for the surprise baby shower Autumn and his mother were throwing for Hannah.

Garrett was in charge of taking her to church and then coming up with a reason to delay his taking her home to give everyone time to get to his place before her. He couldn't wait to see the look on her face when she realized the party was for her. But he was even more anxious to see her response when she saw the surprise he had for her.

He watched as she rinsed off a plate, handing it to him to dry with a cheery smile. Neither of them had brought up the talk they'd had the night they'd come home from the rodeo. What more was there to say? She wasn't at a point where she felt comfortable moving to Bent Creek with her son and leaving her father in Steamboat Springs all alone. And Garrett couldn't just pick up and leave his brothers to run the business without him. He'd prayed about it, but no amount of praying was going to change those facts. Nor would her leaving change the feelings he'd come to have for her. Just as he'd had to do with Grace, he would lock those feelings away, and go on with his life as he'd been living it before Hannah had come into it. Emotionally alone.

Clearing his throat, before emotion got the better of him, Garrett cast a quick glance at the LED clock display on the stove's panel. "We'd best get a move on."

"Almost done," Hannah said as she rinsed the remaining suds off the two forks she held in her hand. Then she turned, handing them over to him. "Here you go. While you dry those and put them away, I'll go grab my purse."

Nodding, Garrett placed the forks in a dish towel and began to dry them.

Hannah paused, looking up at him with a tender smile, the sight of which had the beat of his heart kicking up a notch or two. Clearly the uncooperative organ forgot that it was Sunday, a day for relaxation, not for skittering about wildly just because Hannah had blessed him with one of her sweet smiles. "I really am going to miss being here," she said, her green eyes misting over. "Thank you for being my friend."

He wanted to be so much more. "Always," he said, determined to make her last few days there ones she would always remember, starting with the surprise he had for her that afternoon.

"Surprise!" The word rose up around Hannah in multitude, and from all around her, the second she and Garrett stepped into his house.

Hannah looked past the opening that led into the living room to see Garrett's family standing in front of the fireplace, smiles on their faces. Blue and white crepe paper was draped across the thick wood mantel, while a dozen or so matching balloons swayed to and fro on each side of the fireplace.

She looked to Garrett. "It's your birthday?" Why hadn't he said something? Thankfully, he'd needed to drop off the bread and milk he'd picked up after church before leaving for the hospital, or he would have been a no-show for this wonderful surprise birthday party his family had planned for him.

"This party isn't for me," Garrett replied, his green eyes twinkling. "It's for you."

"What?" It wasn't her birthday.

"Mom and Autumn wanted to throw you a

surprise baby shower before you went back to Colorado," he explained.

"And me!" Blue exclaimed from where she stood holding Tucker's hand.

"And Blue," Garrett said with a chuckle.

Hannah's gaze shifted back to the gathering of grinning Wades in the adjoining room. The blue streamers and balloons that surrounded them had been meant for her. Tears filled her eyes as Emma and Autumn stepped forward to greet her.

"Well, I'm certainly surprised," Autumn said, the words catching on the emotion building in her throat as Garrett's mother leaned in to give her a hug. "But you shouldn't have gone to all this trouble. You've done more than enough for me already."

"It was no trouble," Autumn assured her as she stepped in for her turn to give Hannah a hug.

"Not at all," Emma said in agreement. "We had so much fun planning this baby shower."

"They weren't about to send you home without one," Garrett told her.

"Not a chance," Autumn acknowledged with a bright smile. "You're gonna have your hands full with a newborn once you get home. We didn't want you to have to worry about running out to pick up the essentials you're gonna be needing."

"We got you lots of presents!" Blue piped in, her tiny voice carrying across the room.

Hannah felt the sting of tears in her eyes. "Thank you."

Emma Wade smiled warmly. "No tears. This is a happy occasion. Now come on in and greet your guests."

She followed Garrett's mother into the living room, intending to thank Garrett's father and brothers for joining in on that afternoon's festivities, but stopped short as her gaze was drawn to the occupied folding chairs that had been placed along the wall to her left on each side of the sofa table that sat below the front window. Her guests, women Hannah had met through Emma at Sunday services, smiled back at her, uttering words of greeting and congratulations.

"Thank you all for being part of this," Hannah said. "I feel so blessed."

"You are," a familiar voice said. "With a very special little boy."

She turned to find Jessica grinning up at her from the sofa on the opposite side of the room.

"Agreed," Autumn said as she moved to take a seat at the other end of the sofa.

"Jessica?" Hannah muttered, pleasantly surprised, yet shocked to see her there.

Her friend gave a small wave. "Surprise!"

"I thought you might like having her be a part of your special day," Garrett said behind her.

Like Autumn and Emma, Jessica had become a good friend. "Yes," Hannah replied. "Thank you so much for including her." Her gaze traveled about the room and her vision blurred with tears. "I'll never forget all the kindness I've been shown during my stay here in Bent Creek."

"We should get started," Emma said, stepping back into the living room.

Jackson pushed away from where he'd been leaning back against the fireplace. "Guess that means it's time for us men to go do 'man' things while you ladies do whatever it is you all do at baby showers."

Tucker and Grady were right on Jackson's heels, clearly anxious to take their leave from the room filled with women.

"You coming?" Tucker asked Garrett on his way past his brother.

"Not until Hannah opens his gift," their mother said.

"You got me something?" she said, looking up at him, not having expected that. But then she hadn't expected any of this, the party, the kindhearted women who had come to celebrate her son's birth.

"Just a little something I thought Austin might like." His gaze shifted toward the window and then back to her. "I had something else I had hoped to surprise you with, but it's going to have to wait."

"Garrett," she chided, "you didn't have to get me anything."

He smiled. "I wanted to."

"Hannah, honey," Garrett's mother said, "why don't you go ahead and have a seat on the sofa to open your gifts? Afterward, we'll have finger sandwiches and cake."

"Your homemade cranberry-walnut-chicken salad sandwiches?" Garrett asked his mother.

His mother smiled. "That and egg salad sandwiches which Autumn and Blue made."

"We put it inside half-moon sandwiches," Blue informed him.

He looked to Autumn who laughed softly. "Croissants," she explained with a grin. "Thus the 'half-moon.'"

He nodded in understanding. "Of course," he said, looking to Blue. "Those are my favorite."

"Mine, too," Hannah said with a smile as she settled onto the sofa between Jessica and Autumn. She turned to give Jessica a quick hug. "Thank you for coming," she said softly.

"I wouldn't have missed it for the world," her friend replied, reaching out to give Hannah's hand a squeeze.

Garrett crossed the room to a gift-laden table,

one Hannah had failed to notice when she'd first entered. Then again, her attention had been drawn to all the people gathered there. She watched as he picked up a large, misshapen package from the floor by the table, one that had been wrapped in a bright red, oversize gift bag, and carried it over to where she sat waiting.

"Little something?" she repeated as she eyed the not-so-little package he had just placed on the floor in front of her.

"It could have been a real one," he said with a grin as she opened the bag.

"Garrett," she said as she pushed the plastic covering away to reveal an old wooden rocking horse. One with such fine detail and craftsmanship that Hannah had to assume it had been handmade.

"There wasn't time to order a new rocking horse," Garrett hurried to explain, "so I thought I would give Austin mine."

She ran her fingers appreciatively over the horse's braided rope mane. "This belonged to you?" It was hard to imagine a man Garrett's size ever being small enough to ride the wooden horse. She was about to tell him he needed to keep something that special for his own child, but then remembered he would never have a child of his own.

"It most certainly did," his mother said, drawing everyone's attention her way. "My son nearly rocked a hole right through his bedroom floor when he was little, he loved that thing so much. Born to ride, he was."

"You don't have to keep it," he said, sounding almost anxious about the gift he'd given her. "We can order Austin a new one and have it sent to Steamboat Springs. I just thought he ought to have a horse of some sort, seeing as how he was born on a horse ranch."

Hannah smiled up at him. "It means so much more to me that this horse belonged to you. If it weren't for you, I might not be sitting here today. And my son…" She let the words trail off, unable to even speak them.

"I'm glad you like it," he said.

Hannah nodded, her smile returning. "I do. And thank you for choosing to go with a wooden horse as opposed to a real live flesh-and-blood one. Taking care of a newborn is going to keep me busy enough."

A warm chuckle passed through his lips. "You're welcome."

"My turn!" Blue announced as she skipped over to the present table.

"She's in charge of bringing you your gifts to unwrap," Autumn explained.

"I can't think of a better present-helper to have

than Blue," Hannah said, earning a toothy grin from her little helper.

"Time for me to make my exit," Garrett said. "You ladies enjoy the party."

The second he stepped from the room, Hannah's gaze shifted over to Blue who was lifting, with great effort, a neatly wrapped present topped with curling strands of multicolored ribbon.

Blue turned, wobbling slightly as she carried the elongated box over to Hannah. "I picked this out all by myself," Blue told her.

"Then I'm sure it's going to be very special," Hannah replied, taking the offered gift. The weight of it surprised her. "Whatever could this be?" she said, enjoying the delight on Blue's face as she worked the ribbons off one end of the wrapped box. "A real horse, perhaps?"

Blue giggled. "A horse can't fit in a box."

"No," Hannah said, "I suppose not. Well, let's see then…" She peeled the paper away. "A swing," she announced, holding it up for the other women in the room to see.

"It's just like mine," Blue said excitedly.

Autumn nodded. "Just like her uncle Garrett loved his rocking horse, Blue loves her swing."

"You gotta tie it to a tree," Blue explained, her gaze fixed on the gift in Hannah's lap.

"I will have to find the perfect tree to hang it

from," Hannah said as Blue hurried over to get her another gift to unwrap.

Once the gift opening was done and the delightful luncheon Autumn and Emma had prepared for the shower all eaten, Hannah went around personally thanking her guests. When the door closed behind the last of the ladies from the church who had come that afternoon, Hannah hurried over to help Emma and Autumn with the cleanup.

"Thank you both for the surprise shower," she told them as she gathered up empty paper cups.

Autumn smiled. "We're glad you enjoyed yourself."

The sound of the front door opening drew Hannah's gaze that way. A second later, Garrett appeared in the living room entryway, grinning like she had never seen him grin.

She looked at him questioningly.

"Remember that other gift I mentioned?"

"Yes," she said with a nod.

"They've arrived."

Her brows drew together. "They?"

He inclined his head in the direction from which he'd just come. "Come see."

Hannah set the stack of cups she'd collected down onto a nearby end table and then followed him from the room.

Garrett lifted Hannah's spring jacket from the

hall tree by the door and helped her into it. Then, with his grin still intact, turned to open the front door, motioning her outside.

She'd barely taken two steps out onto the porch when a bark sounded, followed immediately by another. Barks she knew. With a gasp, Hannah spun around, her gaze landing on her father who stood smiling at her from the yard, a leash held securely in each hand. At the end of those leashes, her beloved dogs jumped and tugged at the nylon straps, barking excitedly.

"Daddy!" she exclaimed.

"Hello, baby girl," he called back. "Sorry we missed the party. It took longer than I thought to get here."

Tears streaming down her cheeks, Hannah started across the porch in quickened steps. Garrett's steadying hand close around her arm as she reached the edge of the porch.

"They're not going anywhere," he assured her as he helped her down the steps, something Hannah was grateful for as her legs suddenly felt as wobbly as Jell-O. "No need to risk taking a tumble down the steps."

Her father moved toward the house, the energetic, young golden retrievers eagerly towing him.

There was no way she was going to get to hug her father until she'd acknowledged her whimpering pups. "Buddy," she said as she bent to receive a wet kiss. She gave him a loving scratch behind his long, floppy ears and then turned to acknowledge Bandit, giving him a quick hug. "I've missed you boys so much," she said, her voice catching.

"What about me?" her father teased.

She straightened, her dogs still vying for her attention.

"I've got them," Garrett said, taking the leashes from her father who immediately gathered Hannah in his arms.

Tears rolled down her cheeks as she hugged him back. "I've missed you so much. I'm so happy to see you."

"I've missed you, too, baby girl," her father replied, his voice cracking ever so slightly. "I wish I could have been here sooner."

"You were sick," she said with an empathetic smile. "I'm just thankful you're finally over that awful virus."

"That makes two of us," he agreed. "When Garrett called to see how I was feeling, as he's done several times since you arrived in Bent Creek, he asked me if there was any chance I could make it to the surprise baby shower they were having for you after church today. I knew I couldn't miss it."

She looked to Garrett in surprise. "You've

been talking to my father?" How could he have kept that from her?

"A few times a week, and I called him first," her father clarified. "You gave me Garrett's number in case I couldn't reach you on your phone. I wanted to make sure you weren't keeping things from me. Especially, since I haven't been able to get here to see how you and my grandson are doing for myself."

"I've told you everything there is to know," she said in her own defense, and then realized she hadn't told him *everything*. She hadn't mentioned anything to her father about her feelings for Garrett. Hadn't even told Garrett how much she cared for him. That she was falling in love with him. But that was for the best, seeing as how they would soon be living miles apart from each other.

"Honey, you and I both know you tend to sugarcoat things nowadays where I'm concerned. But I'm a lot stronger than you think I am."

"I think we're both stronger than either of us realize," Hannah admitted.

Her father nodded.

"I wasn't trying to go behind your back," Garrett said, drawing her attention his way. A troubled frown pulled at his mouth. "Just trying to assure your father that you and Austin were both doing well, which is the truth. Then our conversations would go to everyday things, including sharing a little bit about each of our lives."

How could she hold it against Garrett that he'd kept this from her? When the secret she withheld from him, the fact that she had fallen in love with him, could be far more life altering. "I'm not upset with you. Just surprised."

"Understandable," her father said. "But know that I am beyond grateful for the conversations Garrett and I have had. The house has been far too quiet. At least, it is when the dogs are outside playing. More important, our talks gave me the chance to get to know him better, and his family through him. They were caring for my baby girl after all."

"Oh, Dad," Hannah said with a sad smile. "I'm sorry you've had to be alone."

"It's not like you had a choice in the matter," he told her with an affectionate smile. "I'm just thankful the good Lord has more planned for you and my grandson in this life."

She nodded, saying softly, "So am I."

"It's been tearing me apart," he went on, his expression pained, "knowing I was finally well enough to come to Bent Creek to be with you and my grandson, but unable to find a kennel to take Buddy and Bandit until the end of next week."

"If I had known that was what was keeping

your father from coming here, I would have said something earlier," Garrett said, shaking his head. "He never made mention of it until I called to see if he was able to come sooner than you expected him to be here."

"Garrett insisted I bring Buddy and Bandit with me. That you were missing not only me, but your boys as well." Her father looked to Garrett with a grateful smile. "And here we are."

Garrett looked her way. "If you had told me that was why your father hadn't been able to come after having been cleared by his doctor to travel, I would have told you the same thing."

"I didn't want to burden you any more than I already have," she told him.

"Hannah," Garrett said, his tone lightly scolding, "you are not, nor have you ever been, a burden to me. And this is a ranch. A dog or two added to the rest of our animal menagerie of horses, chickens and cats is no big deal. Your happiness is."

Hannah felt her father watching her, but couldn't look his way, knowing that if she did he'd see the truth of her feelings for Garrett written on her face. "Thank you for that," she said, kneeling to give more attention to her pups. "Having my boys here, having my father here, makes me beyond happy." She lifted her gaze, finding Garrett's warm smile. "Thank you for making this day even more special than it already was. I'll never forget everything you've done for me." And she would never forget him. Ever.

"I can't wait for you to meet your grandson," Hannah said as she and her father stepped away from the desk where they had signed him in and moved toward the NICU doors. Garrett had driven them there as soon as they'd gotten her dogs settled in at his place. Not that it had taken much effort. Buddy and Bandit had made themselves right at home on the rug in front of Garrett's fireplace and were napping within minutes.

"I can't wait to meet him," her father replied with a grin as he placed the sterile mask over his nose and mouth and drew the elastic string back over his head.

"Your doctor cleared you to see Austin," Hannah said. "You don't have to wear that."

"I'm not taking any chances," he replied.

Nodding in understanding, she led him to the room that housed the babies needing more specialized care. "Austin is the only baby in here right now."

"I'd say that's a blessing," he replied. "And he gets to come home within the next few days."

They were greeted by the nurse assigned to watch over Austin that afternoon. After introductions were made, Hannah led her father over to the incubator that held his grandson. "Austin, look who I brought to see you. Your grandpa."

Her father placed a flattened hand against the glass, and then cleared his throat before speaking. "I've been waiting for what feels like forever to be able to meet you," he said, his voice cracking. He looked to Hannah, concern knitting his graying brows. "He's so small."

Her smile softened. "Not as small as he was. He's filled out quite a bit since he was first born."

Thick tears looming in his eyes, he looked back to his grandson. "To think what might have happened to the both of you…"

"But it didn't," she said. "That's all that matters."

"I owe Garrett Wade more than I could ever repay him in this lifetime."

"Garrett would never accept any type of repayment for what he's done," she said, knowing that without a doubt. "He risked his life for us because that's the kind of man he is. Brave and caring. And it doesn't end there. He's kind and dependable, and a man of his word." She looked over to find her father studying her.

"You've grown quite attached to this young man," he noted. "And something tells me the sentiment goes both ways."

Garrett had gone from being a stranger to being someone she could confide in. A man she had come to care about. Probably too much if she were being honest with herself. But she couldn't bring herself to admit her feelings aloud. "I've grown attached to the entire Wade family. They've all been so good to me." She looked to her son. "To us."

"I'd like to take a moment to say a prayer of thanks," her father announced, bowing his head.

Hannah closed her eyes and lowered her head as well.

"Thank You, Lord," he began, "for blessing us with this child, a piece of Heather for us to love and to always remember her by. Thank You for bringing Garrett Wade and his family into my daughter's life to watch over Hannah and my grandson when I wasn't physically able to do so. And thank You for allowing Austin's fragile little body to grow and strengthen with each passing day. Amen."

"Amen," Hannah repeated, tears stinging her eyes.

Josie, the nurse on shift, one who had been assigned to Austin when Jessica wasn't there, walked over to join them. "He's doing well," she told them. "No more fussing when it comes to his feedings."

"He's eating already?" her father said in disbelief.

She smiled. "Not actual food. I was referring

to his taking the bottle, something he struggled with at first. But he's come around, taking his formula like the growing little boy he is."

"I wasn't able to nurse him," Hannah admitted, feeling as if she had failed her son. The nurses had stressed to her that this can happen when the mother is overly stressed, which she had been, between the loss of her mother and sister, the flood, and then Austin's early arrival.

"Your mother wasn't able to nurse you or your sister either, and you both turned out okay," her father said with a warm smile.

"I never knew that," Hannah admitted, wondering if it wasn't stress that had affected her milk flow, but something genetic. She knew that if her mother were still alive, she would have shared those sorts of things with her daughters when the time called for it.

"Would you like me to get him out for you so you can hold him?" her son's nurse asked.

Hannah nodded. "Yes, please." She looked to her father. "You can go first. But we have to wash our hands before we can hold him."

"Understandable," her father replied as he followed her over to the sink.

After they had both washed their hands, she led her father to the rocker that sat next to her son's crib.

Once her father was settled comfortably, Josie

removed Austin from the incubator, carefully adjusting his remaining tubes and wires as she settled the baby into his grandfather's outstretched arms. "He just finished eating a little while ago, so he's a little sleepy right now." Her gaze shifted to Hannah. "Let me know when you're ready to change places with your father."

"I will," Hannah said. "Thank you." She turned her attention back to her father who was looking down at his grandson, a mixture of both adoration and grief etched into the lines around his eyes. A feeling Hannah understood all too well. Overwhelming love for her sister's child, and, yet, a deep pain for the knowledge that her sister would never have the chance to be the mother she had always longed to be.

"He has your sister's eyes," her father muttered as the infant stared up at him, his sleepy eyes drifting open and closed.

Hannah looked down with a sad smile. "Yes, he does."

Her father sniffled, clearly overcome by emotion.

She placed her hand on his shoulder. "I miss her, too, Dad. But our focus right now needs to be on getting Austin home, and giving him the happy childhood Heather would have wanted for him."

He looked up at her. "Are you ready for this?"

"I have to be," she answered honestly. "I just pray that I can be the kind of mother Austin deserves."

"You will be every bit the mother your sister would have been," he replied, his gaze dropping down to the babe in his arms. "How could you not be? You were both raised by an incredible woman who exemplified what a mother should be."

Hannah nodded. "She was the best."

"That she was."

Hannah watched her father as he held his grandson, his eyes filled with such love. Rocking slowly, he examined Austin's tiny fingers and toes. Then he smoothed the side of his finger along the infant's baby-soft cheek. "Your grandpa can't wait to have you home with him." He glanced up at Hannah, adding with a tender smile, "Both of you."

Garrett looked up from the magazine he'd been skimming through as Hannah's father stepped into the waiting room that sat just outside of the NICU's doors.

The older man made his way over to Garrett who was rising to his feet to greet him. "Your turn."

"My turn?" He'd driven them to the hospital

but hadn't counted on getting to visit Austin with only two visitors being allowed.

"I thought you might want to go in and see Austin. Hannah tells me you've formed a special bond with my grandson."

Garrett couldn't deny that he felt a deep emotional connection to Hannah's son. With Hannah, too. They'd been through so much together in the weeks since the flood. "I can't answer for Austin, but I can tell you that he's definitely touched a big part of my heart." Just as his mother had.

"Then why don't you go on in and see him?" James Sanders suggested.

"I wouldn't feel right taking time away from your seeing him," Garrett said honestly.

Hannah's father smiled. "I have a lifetime to spend with my grandson after we take him home. I think I can share a little time with you while we're here."

Garrett glanced in the direction of the NICU doors. While he'd known Hannah would be leaving and taking her son with her, hearing her father talk about it really made it hit home.

"Garrett," her father said, drawing his gaze back his way. "I know I've already expressed my gratitude for everything you've done for Hannah and my grandson when you called to tell me about the shower, but words don't seem to be enough. Not for all that you've done."

"I'm just grateful the good Lord set me on the path I was on that day the flood struck," Garrett replied.

"Be that as it may," Hannah's father said, "you are the one who risked his life to save my daughter and her unborn child. You are the one who got them safely to the hospital when the storm rendered the main road impassable. And you are the one who has given Hannah emotional support when I wasn't here to do so. I don't know what I would have done if I'd lost them, too," he said, his voice cracking. "So, if there's ever anything I can do for you, all you have to do is ask."

Garrett hesitated, his heart pushing him to open up to James. To at least try to work something out before the woman he loved drove away with not only his heart, but with the child he'd grown so very fond of. He cleared his throat, gathering up his nerve. "There is something," he told the older man. "I'm just not sure how to approach this."

James Sanders motioned to the empty waiting room seats. "Have a seat, son. Then you can approach whatever it is you have to say the same way you live your life. With honesty, and good measure of faith thrown in."

Garrett sank down onto one of the paddcd

chairs and waited until Hannah's father had taken the seat beside his before saying, "I love your daughter."

"Well, that's getting right to the point," James teased. "But it's nothing I haven't already figured out."

"You knew?" Garrett said, shocked by the older man's response.

"Son, I knew something was building between you and my daughter by our third phone call. And you aren't the only one who wore their feelings on their sleeve when I talked to them. My daughter is quite taken by you to say the least."

"I'd like to ask Hannah to marry me," he announced, his heart pounding. "And I'd like to ask for your blessing."

James studied him for a moment before saying, "The two of you haven't known each other for very long. Are you sure about this?"

"I've never been more certain of anything in my life," Garrett replied. "And I can't blame you for questioning my feelings for your daughter. I would do the same thing if I were in your shoes. But what I feel for Hannah is beyond anything I've ever felt before. And we've spent hours, days, weeks, getting to know each other. I know what her hopes and dreams are, and I know her fears. We share the same faith and family values."

When James said nothing, just stood there watching him, the knot of anxiety in Garrett's gut grew, but he went on, needing Hannah's father to understand how very much he had come to love his daughter. "I've seen how incredibly brave and strong your daughter can be in the face of adversity. I've watched her with her son, knowing without any doubt that she was put on this earth to be a mother. When I think about Hannah going back to Colorado, I know without a doubt that she'll be taking my heart with her." A heart he never thought would feel again after losing Grace.

"I don't like to speak ill of people," James began, making Garrett wonder what he was about to say, "but I don't think Hannah's first husband ever fully appreciated those qualities in my daughter."

"He gave up someone truly special," Garrett said.

"She reminds me so much of her mother."

His heart went out to the man for the loss of his wife, the woman James had spent so many years loving, had raised a family with, had given his heart to. It had been hard enough for Garrett when he'd lost Grace, and they had barely begun to share all of life's experiences together. He just prayed that if Hannah agreed to marry him they would be blessed with a long, happy, marriage, just as their parents had been. "I'm sorry I never had the chance to meet Hannah's mother. I would like to have asked for her blessing, too."

The older man glanced heavenward and then back to Garrett. "Something tells me she would have happily given it to you. Your love for my daughter is evident, son. I could hear it in your voice every time you called to give me an update on Hannah and my grandson. I see it on your face whenever the two of you are together. Her face as well," he said, emotion thick in his voice. "My daughter deserves the happiness she was denied in her first marriage, and, after getting to know you over the past several weeks, I believe in my heart that she can have that with you. But Hannah wouldn't be bringing just herself into any long-term relationship. She'll be bringing Austin."

"Your grandson snagged a huge piece of my heart from the first moment I held him in my arms. I would feel blessed to be able to raise that little boy as my son. And, just so you know, I'm going to ask Hannah to marry me, but I don't intend to rush her into setting a wedding date. I know there are some things we need to work out first, but I'm more than willing to wait until the time is right for her. And for you. Because you are a very big part of what I hope will be our future."

"I would be proud to have a man like you as my son-in-law," James said with a smile, "so I'm giving you my blessing. But the decision is Hannah's to make."

"That means a lot to me," Garrett said with the utmost sincerity, because Hannah's father could one day be his father, too, if everything worked out as he prayed that it would.

Chapter Ten

The entire family had gathered on Garrett's parents' front porch to welcome Hannah home with her newborn son. Or, at least, welcome her to what had been her temporary home during her stay there. A stay that ended with Austin's release from the hospital. Hannah and her father were leaving to go back to Steamboat Springs the following morning. But not for good if Garrett had his way.

He helped Hannah down from the backseat of his truck where she had been seated next to her son, who was tucked securely inside his brand-new car seat. The one his mother and father had bought for the baby. Her father was already on his way to the house, carrying the bag of baby items they'd brought home from the hospital, including the stuffed bear with the bright blue ribbon his brothers had bought for the baby right after Austin was born.

"I'm sorry about this," he said, inclining his head toward the house. "I should have thought to tell them to give you a little bit of breathing room when we got home."

"I don't mind," Hannah replied as she turned to get her son from the car seat. Other than a few coos to Austin during their drive home, they were the first words she'd spoken since leaving the hospital.

"Let me," Garrett told her. "It's a bit of a reach for you from where you're standing."

Stepping aside, she waited as Garrett leaned in to unlatch the safety belt that held her son in, and then gently lifted him from the car seat.

"Everything okay?" he asked as he turned to place the tiny, sleeping bundle into Hannah's outstretched arms.

She smiled, but Garrett could tell it was forced, and he found himself hoping that she was as troubled by her leaving as he was. "A little anxious," she replied. "I'm about to be someone's mother all by myself."

"You won't be alone," he told her as he closed the truck door. Then, wrapping a supportive arm around her waist, they started across the yard. "You'll have your father. And you'll have us."

"I know," she said with a sigh. "And I'm so

grateful to have you all in my life. But knowing that this precious child will be dependent on me now for his every need, to give him guidance, to assure his happiness, and to do things I don't even know I'm supposed to be doing as a mother, is a little daunting."

Her silence on the way home made much more sense to him now that she had told him what was troubling her. He smiled down at her. "You are and will continue to be an incredible mother, Hannah Sanders. Don't you doubt that for even a second."

"The baby's here! The baby's here!" Blue squealed as she bounced down the porch steps and hurried across the yard to meet them.

Garrett chuckled. "Ready to face your welcome committee?"

Hannah nodded, this time with a genuine smile. "As ready as I'll ever be."

Tucker jogged after his daughter, catching up to her not quite halfway across the yard, and swept Blue up into his arms. Then he turned and waited for Autumn who was trailing after them.

"But I wanna see the baby," Blue whined as she peered at the bundle in Hannah's arm from over top her father's shoulder.

"We will," Autumn said. "But we have to wait for Grandma and Grandpa, and Uncle Jackson, so we can meet Austin together."

His parents caught up to them with Jackson moving in unhurried strides behind them.

Garrett's family formed a human circle around Hannah and him, effectively blocking out the chilly breeze. James Sanders stood a few feet away, grinning as he watched the excitement his grandson was causing.

"I can't see him," Blue muttered with a frustrated frown as she looked down at the bundle from her perch in her father's arms.

Smiling, Hannah peeled the blanket away from her son's face, just enough to give everyone a peek at her son without exposing him fully to the crisp fall air.

Blue let out a little gasp. "He looks like a baby doll."

"Give him a few months," Garrett said with a chuckle.

"Oh, my," his mother sighed, a hand going to her heart. "He's beyond precious."

Garrett's father leaned in for a closer look. With a nod, his gaze lifted to Hannah's. "Looks like you have yourself a fine, strapping son."

Her smile widened. "Hopefully, he will grow up to be as strapping and kindhearted as your sons."

"He's named after one of them," his father replied. "How can he grow up to be anything but?"

Autumn, who stood next to Hannah, reached

out to run a fingertip along the baby's cheek. "He's so perfect," she said, her eyes misting over. "And seeing you holding your son makes me wish that I were already holding our baby in my arms." Her softly spoken words of longing immediately drew everyone's gaze her way.

"Baby?" Jackson repeated, looking to Tucker.

"Baby?" his mother repeated, her face lighting up.

Their little brother looked to his wife, one lone brow lifting.

Autumn giggled and, with a shrug of her slender shoulders, said, "Oops."

Grinning, Tucker shook his head. "It appears the cat's out of the bag. Autumn and I were going to wait until Thanksgiving to tell everyone our good news."

"Why did you put a cat in a bag, Daddy?" Blue asked as she stood looking up at him.

Jackson snorted. "I was wondering the same thing myself."

Tucker shot him a warning glance. "Just wait until the shoe is on the other foot."

"Never going to happen," their brother said, some of the humor leaving his face.

"Never say never," their father muttered, no doubt having taken stances in his life that he hadn't been able to hold firm to.

Garrett had done the same himself, vowing

to never love again after losing Grace. But here he was, head-over-cowboy-boots in love with Hannah.

Blue's brows creased in confusion. "Why would Uncle Jackson wear his shoes on the wrong feet? That would hurt."

Garrett's mother laughed. "I think we need to take this conversation inside, so Hannah can get her son settled in." She looked to Autumn with a delighted smile. "And you can tell us all about your exciting news."

The circle his family had formed around them disbanded as everyone moved into the house. A bassinet had been set up against the wall where the living room opened up to the dining room. That way Hannah could keep an eye on her son during dinner and then afterward when they moved to the living room to share some light-hearted conversation.

"Hannah…" Garrett said when there was a lull in the conversation going on around him.

She looked his way with a soft smile.

"Would you mind taking a walk with me?"

Her gaze automatically went to the bassinet where her son slept.

"He's sound asleep," her father assured her. "Go on and enjoy your walk. I think you have plenty of backup should my grandson awaken before you get back." He looked to Garrett with a nod, and Garrett knew that it was time to lay his heart on the line in hopes of convincing Hannah to place her own heart into his safekeeping.

"It's colder out than I thought," Garrett stated with a frown as they stepped out into the star-lit night, the decorative, battery-operated lantern his mother had given him dangling from his hand.

Hannah snuggled deeper into her coat, her long, coppery hair whipping about in the breeze. "It's the start of spring," she reminded him as they stepped down from the porch, knowing that during that time of year the weather could go from decently warm to raining, or even snowing that same day. And, at that moment, it felt cold enough to snow.

He paused at the base of the steps, looking about with a troubled frown.

"Garrett?"

"Let's go to the barn," he said. "It'll be warm enough there."

"I thought we were going for a walk."

He looked down at her. "We need to talk, and I don't want you standing outside in the cold. Not with the wind kicking up the way it is."

"Garrett, please don't make this any harder than it already is," Hannah pleaded. Ever since he'd admitted to having feelings for her, asking her to give them a chance, and she'd had no choice but to turn him down, her heart had been aching.

"I don't intend to," he said. "But there is something I need to say, and I'd rather do so where it's somewhat warm."

"The house was warm," she said, thinking it might have been best not to have accepted Garrett's invitation for a walk that evening.

"But not private," he replied.

With a nod, she conceded, and then started for the barn, her heart pounding. She didn't want to talk about her leaving. Or about feelings neither of them would ever be able to act upon. And she didn't want to cry, but even now her eyes were tearing up. She could blame it on the brisk breeze, but her heart knew better. She loved Garrett. And she was going to leave him. Not in the same way Grace had, but it tore at Hannah all the same. She didn't want to be the cause of his closing himself off to love again. Garrett deserved to be happy, even if it couldn't be with her. *Lord, please help me to be strong. And please help guide Garrett down a path that allows him to find the happiness he deserves.*

When they entered the barn, Garrett closed the large door and then turned to face her, his gaze meeting hers. "I had planned to have this discussion out under the stars with the mountains in the backdrop gently lit by the light of the moon. I hadn't counted on a cold front moving in."

A discussion under the stars? And with moonlight on the mountains. That sounded far too romantic a setting for a goodbye. Before she had a chance to dwell on it any further, Garrett closed the distance between them in three long strides and took her hands in his.

"Hannah Sanders," he began, the sound of her name on his lips making her heart race, "you came into my life so unexpectedly. So vulnerable, yet so very strong. From that very first moment when your fearful gaze met mine through that rain-splattered car window, I knew God had placed me there for a reason. What I hadn't realized then was that it was to do more than rescue you from the storm. It was to save me from myself and the emotional isolation I had placed my heart in when it came to ever loving someone again. You made me feel again."

"Garrett," she said with a panicked groan. She couldn't do this. They'd already discussed the reasons why. Tears filled her eyes.

"Hannah, please hear me out," he said tenderly. "The more I came to care for you and Austin, the more I wanted to throw a lasso over time to keep it from moving forward. But that wasn't an option. Telling you that I've fallen in love with you is. I want to marry you and take that trip to see the northern lights you've longed to go on for our honeymoon. And if you want more children, I'm willing to adopt. We can have that large family you've always dreamed of."

A small sob escaped her lips. "Oh, Garrett…"

"I'm not ready to let you walk out of my life without fighting for you," he told her. "Fighting for us."

She shook her head. "We've already been through this. Neither of us is free to move at this point in our lives, and I can't do a long-distance relationship."

He reached for her hands. "What if you don't have to?"

"Garrett, you can't leave the business you've built here with your brothers for me," she told him, despite her heart wishing otherwise.

"If that's what it takes," he said.

He would do that for her? Tears blurred her vision. "I would never let you do that."

"Then we'll make the long-distance thing work until you feel your father can manage on his own," he told her. "I'm willing to wait as long as it takes if it means you'll be a part of my future. Or have him move to Bent Creek with you and Austin. He's retired, so you wouldn't be asking him to leave his job."

"But I would be asking my father to give

up the life he's built in Steamboat Springs, the friends he's made, for me. I can't do that. And I can't take his grandson away from him. Not this soon after losing Mom and Heather," she said, eyes tearing up. "And it wouldn't only be me moving here if I accepted your offer. I have a son that I'll be raising."

"I know that. I want the entire package, you and Austin. How do you feel about raising children and horses?" he countered with a casual shrug, flashing her that charming cowboy grin she'd come to adore.

"Garrett, be serious," Hannah said. Only Garrett could make her want to cry and laugh at the same time.

"I am," he replied, meeting her tear-filled eyes. "And I hope someday to be the man helping you raise your son. I love you, Hannah Sanders, and, at the risk of sounding a little too self-assured, I think you feel the same way about me."

It would be best to put that notion to rest, to tell him that she was grateful for all he had done for her, but nothing more. Only that would be a lie, something she couldn't bring herself to do. "I do love you," she admitted softly. "With all my heart."

His smile widened. A second later, Garrett was kneeling before her, her hand still in his as his free hand slid into the front pocket of his jeans, pulling out a small black box. "Your father has given me his blessing."

Hannah placed her hand over his before he could open the box, tears rolling down her cheeks. "I love you, Garrett Wade. I always will. But I can't accept your proposal. You deserve to find happiness with someone who is free to be with you here in Bent Creek. As much as I want to be that woman, I can't leave my father to deal with his grief alone. And I have no idea how long it will be before I feel comfortable doing so."

Garrett searched her face for a long moment, as if trying to commit it to memory. Then, with a nod of surrender, he stood and released her hand, tucked the ring box back into his jeans pocket. "We'd best get back to the house. I've kept you out here in the cold long enough." He turned, opened the barn door and then reached for the lantern.

Hannah wanted so desperately to throw her arms around Garrett and tell him she was sorry. That she wanted more than anything to be his wife. But life didn't always work out the way one hoped it would. She knew that better than most. Brushing the tears from her cheeks, Hannah stepped out into the night, her heart breaking.

They walked back to the porch in silence. But when they reached his parent's front door, Garrett turned to her. "Just so you know. There will never be another woman for me." That said, he opened the door, the cold wind whipping in behind her, forcing Hannah to step inside before she could respond.

"Back already?" Tucker said when they entered the living room.

"A cold front moved in," Garrett muttered, not meeting Hannah's gaze. He was closing himself off again. She could feel it. And it was all her fault.

"Take off your jackets and warm up by the fire," his mother suggested.

"I have to get going," Garrett announced.

"Already?" Autumn asked in surprise.

"I have a few things I need to do at home yet this evening," he told them.

"Will we see you in the morning?" Hannah asked, not wanting this to be the way they parted ways. With Garrett hurting and her regretting.

He finally looked her way. "I'll be here." With a nod, he bid everyone good-night and then walked out.

Hannah shrugged out of her jacket and draped it over her arm. "I think I'll turn in early tonight."

"Is everything all right, dear?" Emma Wade asked with a worried frown.

"It's been a long day," she told her, forcing a

smile. "I'm tired and should try and get some rest before I have to get up through the night for feedings."

Her father pushed out of the chair he'd been sitting in. "You get Austin. I'll carry the bassinet upstairs for you."

Nodding, Hannah walked over to where her son lay sleeping and eased her hands beneath his tiny, blanket-bundled form, gently lifting him. Then she turned and thanked Garrett's family for all they had done for her and her son during their stay there.

"We'll be here to see you off tomorrow," Autumn said. "So, I'm going to save my goodbyes for then."

The others nodded in agreement.

Tears pooled in her eyes. "Good night then." Hannah carried her son up the stairs, her father, carrying the bassinet, followed behind her.

"What happened between you and Garrett?" he asked, the moment they entered the guest bedroom where Hannah had been staying.

"I don't know what you mean," she said, unable to look her father in the eye. He knew her too well. He would see her pain.

He placed the bassinet beside the bed and then turned to her. "I was expecting you and Garrett to come back to the house with an announcement. Not part ways like neither of you could bear to look at one another."

"I told Garrett no," she replied, a tear rolling down her cheek.

Her father's brows drew together in confusion. "Why? That young man's heart is overflowing with love for you. I thought you felt the same way about him. Was I mistaken?"

"No," she said with a sniffle. "You weren't."

"So you do you love him?"

She nodded. "Yes."

"Then why did you turn his proposal down? Is this about what happened with Dave?" he asked with a frown. "Because Garrett isn't anything like your ex."

Lifting her gaze, she said sadly, "No, it has nothing to do with Dave."

"I know your relationship with Garrett happened faster than most do, but I believe it's real."

She walked over to place her sleeping son into the bassinet. "It's not just about Garrett and me. There are others to consider. He can't just up and leave his brothers and the business they run together. Although, he offered to give it all up for me. And there's you."

"Me?" he said with a lift of his slightly graying brows.

"Dad, I can't leave you alone in Steamboat Springs," she admitted. "Not now."

"You gave up your chance at happiness with Garrett so I wouldn't be alone?"

Tears ran down her cheeks. "You've lost so much already. I won't take your grandson away from you."

He walked over and drew her into his arms for a comforting hug, resting his chin on the top of her head. "Honey, all I want is for you to be happy, something you won't be back in Steamboat Springs. Not only because Garrett won't be there, but because our home isn't really home anymore. Not without your mother there."

She lifted her head to look up at him questioningly.

"What would you say if I told you that I'd like a fresh start somewhere else?" he asked as he released her and took a step back.

"You would leave Steamboat Springs?" she asked in disbelief. "Where would you go?"

"I was kind of thinking Bent Creek would be a nice place to begin anew," he said with a smile. "Especially, since my daughter and grandson will be living here."

"But you'd be leaving the home you and Mom made so many memories in."

"Memories can be taken with you anywhere," he said with a wistful smile. "I'd like to find a smaller place with a little bit of land, maybe even get a dog, because Bandit and Buddy will be moving out when you do, and start making new memories for myself. More important," he said, "I want you to find the same happiness I found with your mother. And for that to happen you need to follow your heart."

Her father's words were the answer to her prayers. She would no longer be forced to choose between the two men she loved most in the world. She could follow her heart, knowing right where it would lead her—to the kind, loving cowboy who had come to her rescue and had shown her what true love really was.

Garrett pulled up to his parents' house, his gaze immediately drawn to Hannah who was sitting alone on the front porch. She wore a sweater and a denim jacket, but the way she was hugging herself told him Hannah was still chilled.

Cutting the engine, he stepped out of his truck and strode toward the porch. "It's a little cold to be sitting outside," he remarked.

"I was waiting for you," she said, a hint of uneasiness in her voice. She stood and made her way down the porch steps until she stood in front of him on the walkway. "I thought we could take a walk."

A frown tugged at his mouth. He knew what the walk she wanted to take was about. She wanted to tell him goodbye in private. Maybe so he wouldn't cause a scene like he had the night before when he'd left so abruptly. "About last night," he said. "I'm sorry I left the way I did."

"I'm sorry I hurt you," she replied. "I tried to call you last night, but I couldn't reach you. Not that I blame you for not picking up the phone."

"It wasn't on purpose," he told her. "I set my cell phone on the kitchen counter last night after I got home, and then went outside to sit and think for a while. I didn't see that I had missed your call until this morning. My first thought was that something was wrong with Austin. But my brothers would have come to get me if that were the case. Not sure what else there is for you and I to say this morning other than goodbye." It hurt even speaking the words. He didn't want her to leave—ever.

"Let's take that walk," she said with a smile that made his heart yearn.

He had to be the man his mother had raised him to be and tuck his hurt and frustration away. With a nod, they started away from the porch. "At least, the wind isn't whipping about today."

"It wouldn't matter," she told him. "We're going to the barn."

The pain dug a little deeper. The last place he wanted to be with her was the place where Hannah had put an end to his hopes and dreams of a future together with her. "Okay," he conceded in silent suffering.

They crossed the yard and stepped into the barn, only this time it was Hannah who closed the door behind them. Then she turned to look up at him. "I have to leave this morning," she told him.

He nodded knowingly, his mouth pressed into a firm line.

"But only to go back and give notice to my job and help my father get the house ready to put up for sale."

It took a long moment for her words to settle in. "You what?"

"Garrett Wade," she said, her nervous smile softening, her beautiful green eyes searching his, "you are everything I could ever want in a husband. You're compassionate, strong of faith and a devoted family man—one I'd love to raise my son with. So, if your offer of marriage still stands, and you don't mind my father moving to Bent Creek to be near us, then my answer is yes. I would love nothing more than to marry you."

He had spent all night preparing himself for their goodbye, praying to the Lord to watch over Hannah and her son. Now it seemed he might have the privilege of watching over them himself for the rest of their lives together. Joy filled his heart and spread through him.

"If you've changed your mind, I understand," she said, worry replacing her confident smile.

The softly spoken words had him drawing her to him. Looking down at the woman he held in his arms, Garrett smiled. "Not a chance. You are the woman I want to spend the rest of my life with. As your husband, and as the father of your son."

"And you're okay with my father moving here?"

"More than okay," he told her. "I suppose we should go inside and share our good news."

"My father already knows," she admitted. "And I have a feeling your family knows now, too."

He chuckled. "You're probably right."

She leaned into him. "I love you, Garrett Wade."

"I love you, too, Hannah Wade," he replied, his heart filled with it.

Laughing softly, she said, "My name's not Wade yet."

"Just testing it out," he said with a grin.

"It sounds perfect to me," she sighed happily.

"No, you are," he told her. "The perfect woman for me. Thank you for giving me the family I never thought I'd have."

"Thank you for making my family complete," she replied, tears in her eyes.

Emotion welling up inside him, Garrett lowered his mouth to hers in a tender kiss, one that promised a lifetime of love and devotion.

* * * * *